Dig Ten Graves

Stories by Heath Lowrance

Copyright 2021, Heath Lowrance/Raccoon Books

Cover design and Raccoon Books logo: Meagan Costea

"It Will All Be Carried Away" first appeared in CHIZINE, 2010

"Emancipation, with Teeth" first appeared in NECROTIC TISSUE, 2009

"The Bad Little Pet" first appeared at THE NAUTILUS ENGINE, 2011

"Bleed Out," "From Here to Oblivion," "Gator Boy," "Incident on a Rain-Soaked Corner," "The Most Natural Thing in the World," "Always Too Late," and "Heart" are all original to this collection

Contents:

A Brief Word

It Will All Be Carried Away

Bleed Out

Emancipation, with Teeth

From Here to Oblivion

Gator Boy

Incident on a Rain-Soaked Corner

Always Too Late

The Most Natural Thing in the World

Heart

The Bad Little Pet

A Brief Word

Bear with me just a moment if you will, friend. I'm anxious for you to read these stories, but there are just a couple of things I'd like to say by way of preface. Cool?

This collection, DIG TEN GRAVES, was originally self-published ten years ago, in 2011 (this is the first time I've typed that fact, and holy shit, TEN YEARS?). It came on the heels of my first published novel, THE BASTARD HAND, from New Pulp Press, which at the time was one of the premier small presses specializing in dark and/or transgressive crime fiction.

A few years ago, for various reasons, I made the decision to pull all my work from print. Explaining why would take up way too much of our precious time, and I'm sure your interest in that is minimal at best anyway. But the intention was always to start fresh, when I felt ready to do so.

So here's the fresh start, nearly ten years to the month after my career as a professional writer began.

This time around, the collection represents the first of three volumes of short stories that you'll see over the course of the year, leading up to the republication of THE BASTARD HAND.

I've resisted the urge to tweak these stories too much, aside from some basic edits. The world has changed a lot in the last ten years, and some of the references don't hit the mark the way they used to, but in the end I opted to leave them more or less as they were, as testament, if not to the time and place, then to who I was as a writer in those early days.

I guess that's all.

Let's start digging, shall we?

It Will All Be Carried Away

I read in the paper this morning that Charon was dead. Somewhere in the back pages, just a two paragraph story with the header WOMAN OVERDOSES, FOUND IN BACKSEAT OF CAR, her identity given as Charon Whitfield, age 37, her place of residence some Podunk town fifty miles or so north of Detroit. And that was it. It didn't mention what drug she'd overdosed on, and, what I knew about Charon, it could have been anything.

The name, in bold black letters, Charon Whitfield, nudged something in the back of my brain and it took several seconds before I connected it to the Charon I knew, the Charon who wasn't thirty-seven but seventeen. And then my hands started shaking and I dropped the newspaper on my lap.

On the sofa across the room from me, Sarah looked up from the book she was reading and said, "You okay?" and I nodded. But a tangle of jagged images had washed over me, images of a face I barely remembered, back-lit by the gray light of faded memory.

Charon. Young, weird, sexy Charon. Dead of an overdose. I tried to picture her at thirty-seven and just couldn't get my head around it.

An image flashed in my head, and at the time I couldn't have said where it came from. Charon, think and frail and white, naked. Bound with heavy black cord to a wooden post. People everywhere, strolling past her without even a glance. Naked, bound to a post, struggling to get free, in a store or shop or something.

Like I said, I didn't know right at that moment where the image came from; I'd buried it. Later, I would remember.

I tossed the paper on the coffee table and went into the kitchen. The kids played in the backyard, Sunday morning, and they had the day to do whatever they wanted. Homework done, chores completed, happy happy Sunday, not a care in the world. I poured a cup of coffee, went to the window and stood there watching them for a while.

Anna is ten, Wade seven, and Christ... they're closer to the age I was when I knew Charon than I am now. I was twenty-one, she was seventeen. Too young for me, really, only just legal as they say, but Christ she was a strange one and I can't be sure if what I feel now was what I felt then.

I was a surface fixture then, a good-looking kid with a mouth smarter than his head, a malcontent with a natural instinct to rebel, even though there didn't seem much to rebel against. But beyond the rebellion, beyond the great music and interesting drugs and homemade fashion sense, there were the girls. Lots of girls, if I'm being honest.

I don't even remember most of them. But I do remember Charon. Charon, more than anyone else. Charon, more than any long-term girlfriend or serious relationship or one-nighter. Charon, who occupied a space in my life of three or four months, on and off. Who should have been completely inconsequential, a cheap fuck for those nights when nothing else was going on, a mere phone call away day or night. Who should have been nothing at all.

Charon, age 17, naked and white and frail, bound to a wooden post.

Charon Whitfield, age 37, dead of a drug overdose, found in the backseat of her car.

I'm standing outside the club, smoking a cigarette, when she comes out. She's by herself and she's a little drunk and I perk up right away because I'd noticed her earlier. I'd thought about talking to her but it was getting late and I had to be at my job at ten in the morning. So I'd left, and got caught up just outside the door talking to Kev. Now it's almost three and the parking lot is nearly empty, and still the thumping bass of some song by Ministry strains through the door like a heartbeat.

She comes out by herself. She's wearing black— black leather mini-skirt, black bustier, black fishnet stockings, big black boots— and a vintage purple overcoat with a black fake fur collar. The overcoat hangs comically on her willowy body. Her pageboy haircut is bleach blonde, with black at the roots. Her nose is longish, and her eyes are brown and impossibly huge, like one of those weird Kewpie dolls.

I toss away my cigarette. She glances at me with those crazy big eyes, those dark eyes, and she blinks. She walks on.

All it takes, one glance from those eyes, underscored by black eyeliner, and I must have her.

I trot to catch up to her, and I can't even remember the last time I made even that much effort. A few feet behind her I stop and say, "Hey."

She turns around slowly, almost languidly, and I know right away that's the word I'll always use to describe her: *languid*. She doesn't seem surprised that I've spoken to her. She cocks her head, not smiling but not unfriendly either. She says "Yeah?"

In my mind it takes a million years to come up with something to say, but in reality I speak right away, just a simple, "Are you okay? You seem like something's wrong."

Her voice is deep and lazy and now that she's looking right at me my heart is pounding along with the Ministry song coming from inside and my stomach feels weird. She says, "You're concerned that something's wrong with me? You don't even know me."

"No," I say. "I don't. But yeah, I'm concerned, sure."

She smiles a bizarre crooked smile that doesn't touch any part of her thin face. "Thank you," she says. "Thank you. All I wanted… all I really wanted was for one person to ask me if I was okay. Thank you."

I walked her to her car and we sat in the front seat for a long long time, talking. We smoked a joint, talked some more. By four o'clock in the morning, the club was closing up and the last of the diehards were ambling across the parking lot to their cars to go home, and Charon and I were completely engaged in making out, tongues down each other's throats and my hands under her bustier, fondling her small breasts.

I don't remember anything of what we talked about but eventually the sun sent out its first tendrils of gray light and Charon said, "I really should go," and I said, "Me too," and we made out a little bit more before she gave me her number and I got out of the car and she drove away.

I went home and slept and dreamt about her, dark, sensual dreams, and as soon as I woke up I called her.

I jumped online this afternoon to see if I could find out anything else about her death. The local newspaper for the Podunk town where she'd been found had an article posted.

Charon Whitfield, age 37, was found this morning in the back seat of her car, dead of an apparent drug overdose. The car was parked less than four blocks from the deceased's home.

Investigators say that Ms Whitfield, recently divorced and depressed about the death of her only child earlier this year, apparently took her own life. A needle and other paraphernalia associated with heroin use were found in the vehicle.

Ms Whitfield had spent several years in various drug rehabilitation programs throughout the '90s and early '00s, and co-workers and neighbors said that, despite a long battle against depression and addiction, Ms Whitfield seemed happy and content until the death of her infant daughter from brain cancer. That, and her divorce, investigators say, may have led to her sudden reversal and suicide.

Ms Whitfield leaves no next-of-kin. Funeral services provided by the city will take place on Sunday, March 3, at 9:00 am.

There was a picture taken in 2002, of a woman I didn't recognize. A puffy, used face, mousy brown hair, slack mouth.

The nose, so straight and narrow before, had been broken at some point. Only the eyes looked familiar— huge and dark and innocent.

Funeral services on Sunday, March 3. Today. Her body was found five days ago, and they'd buried her this morning, right about the time I was dragging my creaky body out of bed.

I rubbed my temples, and thought again about that image, the one of Charon, her naked body like a wisp, billowing white smoke, lashed to a wooden post with cord. In the middle of a shop, customers in a buying frenzy, ignoring her as she struggled to get free.

And I remembered where the image came from.

For all the posturing of my cynical youth, I'm not immune to the disease that afflicts middle-aged men, the disease of memory. These days I get up to an alarm clock, never feeling fully rested, to go to a job I hate because, damnit, the bills need to be paid and I have a wife and two kids who count on me. The credit card bills never seem to go down. Sarah's car needs new brakes. Anna wants to go to camp this summer. Our twelfth wedding anniversary is coming up and I promised Sarah that this year we'd go to Hawaii like she always wanted to do. I've promised her this for seven years now.

My back hurts all the time. My vision is getting worse and I'm overdue for a new glasses prescription. I get depressed more often and drinking doesn't make me happy anymore. In fact, if I have more than a few drinks, I get morose and mean-natured.

If I hate that young man I used to be, I hate him because I'm jealous of him.

It's two o'clock in the morning and I'm at Charon's. The place is modest, even a bit run-down. Charon is wearing only panties and a tee-shirt with the Cramps logo on it. Her legs are thin and insanely white and the place smells like vanilla.

"Hey," she says.

Her mom isn't home and it will turn out, over the next few weeks that I know Charon, her mom is never home. Maybe she works nights? Maybe she's always out at a boyfriend's house?

Charon has friends but when I see her, she's always alone.

She doesn't bother to get dressed. I settle in on a ragged sofa and she goes into the kitchen and comes back with a couple of beers. She's seventeen, I find out, and I wonder how she managed to get into the bar, but I don't ask because I never ask anything.

We talk about stuff, nothing important, and she shoves a tape into the VCR and in silence we watch a collection of Siouxsie and the Banshees videos. I've seen most of them before and Charon's proximity to me, her vanilla smell, is driving me nuts but she shoves me away impatiently and says, "I wanna watch this."

So I sip my beer and wait. When the last video on the tape is over, and the final gypsy poundings of "Spellbound" are still lingering in my head, Charon sighs and straddles my lap and we start making out.

In her room, a few minutes later, I finally see all her stuff.

It's a little weird, this bizarre collection of incongruous items. A twelve-inch tall Batman statue, cape unfolded, perches on the nightstand by her bed. The bed itself has a Scooby-Doo bedspread. There's a commemorative plate of Mr. Spock, flanked on either side by a plush doll of Papa Smurf and a plastic see-through horse.

On the other side of the room, one entire wall is lined with things on shelves, very neatly and in some order that doesn't make sense to me. A large crystal ball with the words COME TO

ARIZONA floating inside it. A framed photograph of Stephen King. A toy mouse wearing a pink ribbon on its head, looking up with big loving eyes at a Darth Vader action figure.

Charon takes my hands and leads me to her bed. Her thin fingers trace a line on my chest, under my shirt, and she's nibbling gently at my neck and making a soft moaning sound.

A life-size bust of Nefertiti. An old album cover by Elvis Presley. One of the California Raisins, tiny microphone raised to its wrinkled face.

I pull down her panties and we slide into bed and her body is white and slender in the dim light of the lamp next to her door. She's moving against me, pulsing like a gently revving engine. *She's so… sleek*, I think. Her ribs are symmetrical shadows and I'm strangely aware of her mortality, her thin pulse beating under me.

A scale-model dune buggy with huge wheels. A stuffed raven with a tee-shirt that says Nevermore, already. A toy carousel with pink and baby blue elephants.

I'm kissing her and notice that her eyes are wide open and looking at some vague point above my head. But she bucks her hips against me and I slip off my jeans and she takes me in her hand. She makes an odd little grunting noise but never looks at me.

When I enter her, my eyes have locked onto a lobby card of Christopher Lee as Fu Manchu, taped to the wall.

Sarah took the kids to see their grandmother. I'm supposed to fix the bathroom sink today. It's been clogged up for over a week. There are other chores on my list, but that one is the must-do.

Instead, I log back on the computer and do some research.

I find a posting dated 2004, and it's enough to almost make me stop, it's so horrifying.

But I don't stop. I mark the page to come back to. Three hours later, this is the information I have about the stranger named Charon Whitfield:

She dropped out of high school in 1987 and somehow made her way to California. A photo book about life in L.A. came out in 1988 and there's a picture of Charon in it, a surly-looking little punk rock girl with an orange Mohawk and a blister on her upper lip. The caption reads *Sunset Strip is thronged with punks and other outsiders, begging change from passers-by. Charon, age 18, has only one comment*—"#@**# you".

I find a brief article from a San Francisco newspaper, dated October 1990.

Three homeless people were arrested late last night in connection to an armed robbery that occurred last Friday at the Hazelton Liquor Store on King Avenue. Two of the suspects have warrants outstanding and are being held pending trial. The third, Charon Whitfield, age 19, has no criminal record but is being held for psychiatric evaluation.

And then nothing for a couple of years.

The next thing I find is dated March, 1993. Detroit. Charon managed to find her way home.

Police responded to a complaint early this morning about loud music at 211 Blackmoor Street, a housing development for low-income families, and discovered a young woman who had apparently overdosed on heroin. She was rushed to the hospital, where she is currently listed as being in stable condition.

The woman, Charon Whitfield, age 22, is not a resident of the housing development, but was a 'squatter' who had reportedly been there for some weeks.

Another night, maybe a week, maybe a month, later. We're sprawled out on her bedroom floor, naked and exhausted, sharing a joint, drinking beer. I think I've finally asked her about all the… stuff.

"It's just my stuff," she says, sounding maybe a little defensive. It's the first time I've heard any sort of emotion in her voice.

1996, a headline: WOMAN CONFINED TO PSYCHIATRIC INSTITUTION AFTER DEATH THREATS TO NEIGHBOR.

1997: FORMER MENTAL PATIENT RECOMMITTED AFTER ROBBERY.

1998: SUICIDE ATTEMPT LEADS WOMAN BACK TO MENTAL INSTITUTION.

A notice from 2001 announced her marriage, and a small black and white photo showed her, dark-haired, smiling what seemed like a real smile, and her face looked radiant and happier than I would have ever thought possible. The man at her side was tall and handsome and somewhat sly-looking.

2002, a child born.

Later that same year, a vaguely-worded piece in the police blotter about a domestic disturbance.

And in 2003, the death of her daughter from brain cancer. *Funeral services to be held Friday, August 8. At the request of the bereaved parents, no flowers please. Instead, donations to the Cancer Research Society.*

I couldn't find anything about her divorce. The next bit of information I could find about her, aside from that awful post from 2004, is the article about her death.

Every time I close my eyes now, I see it. All day today, since I learned about her death. I close my eyes and I see her naked, tied to a post, and the shoppers are ignoring her cries, ignoring her struggles, loading their carts.

The second-to-last time I ever saw her, she finally told me about her recurring nightmare.

"I keep having this dream," she says, and her lips feel warm against my neck. We're under a thick quilt on the ragged sofa, and she's fondling me almost absently while she talks. "This nightmare. About my stuff. There's a store, see, a shop. And it's selling all these things and I look and see that it's all mine. It's all of my things that I've collected. And there's all these people and they have shopping carts and bags and stuff and they're loading up with these things that belong to me."

Her fingers had been having an effect on me, but there's something so dreamy and disconnected about her voice now that I lose whatever I'd been building toward. She doesn't seem to notice.

"And I start yelling. Telling them to stop, to leave my stuff alone, it's mine, it's not for sale. And there's a line at the cash register and some fat bitch is ringing them up and they're leaving the store with my things. And suddenly I'm naked, and I'm tied up. Tied to a post with this thick black cord. And I start screaming, leave it alone, leave my stuff alone, it's mine, it's mine, you can't have it!"

For a second her hand tightens on me and I wince. But then she lets go and her fingers rest on my stomach. I feel her eyelashes flutter against my jaw and I'm not sure but I think I feel something hot and wet running down my neck.

"And I'm screaming, it's mine, please, it's all I have, please don't take it. Begging, right. And I'm struggling to get free from this stupid post. And this man, this old man, he stops and looks at me. He's looking at my body, 'cuz I'm naked. He's leering. And he says to me, he says nothing belongs to you, girl. You have nothing. It will all be carried away. So I start crying and pleading, and he laughs and I realize that I recognize him."

Charon is talking rapidly now, still in her bland monotone, and it dawns on me finally that she's revealing something, she's opening up, and I'm not sure if I want her to open up, I'm not sure if I want her fears to rub up next to mine like this. I've been able, so far, to keep myself emotionally removed from her, or so I think. The truth is, I'm already caught up in her, I'm just too self-centered to realize it at the time.

She says, "I recognize him. He's you. He's you, but... old."

The post from 2004. I found it at one of those poetry websites, where anyone can show their work and have it critiqued by fellow poets. I don't know if it was good or bad, and I don't care. By the time I finished it, just a few brief lines, the computer had gone blurry and I couldn't see.

These few possessions

These skins I put on

Are meaningless save for the fact that they are mine

This tender thing I will define as belonging to me

And no one else

But the man who sees me naked

And tied to the post

Will leer and tell me the truth, the ugly truth

That all of this will be carried away

And that in the end, nothing belongs to me

I didn't look at the comments and critiques from the other poets. I don't think I could have stood it if someone tore it apart, critiqued her form or content, reduced it to an exercise.

I see her at the club, about three weeks after she's told me about the dream. She's dyed her hair black. It looks good on her. She doesn't even mention the horrible thing I did, and it dawns on me that she's hopped up on heroin. We find our way to a table far in the back, away from the lights, and make out for awhile and I ask her how she's doing.

She nods and says, "Good, I'm doing good." She smiles and it looks real. She says, "I'm thinking about going to California. I have a friend out there who maybe can get me a job."

I tell her that's great and I wish her luck. I go to get a drink, run into an old girlfriend at the bar, and never go back to Charon's table.

That's the last time I see her.

So now I shut off my computer again and stand up. My back aches and my eyes hurt. I go to the bathroom and look in the mirror and see a man who doesn't really look familiar. He's got lines around his eyes and his Sunday stubble is graying and scraggly. He's got a receding hairline and the beginnings of a double-chin.

I push Charon off me and she almost falls off the sofa and I nearly laugh, she looks so surprised. I pull on my pants and head for the door. Charon, cool collected Charon, never any emotion, has a stunned stupid look on her face. I storm out of the house and to my car, parked in the street. I pop the trunk and find the black extension cord I remembered was there, about fifteen feet of it.

Back in the house. She starts to say, "What are you doing?" but only gets the first word out before I grab her by her thin, frail arm and drag her into the bedroom. She sees the cord and her wide eyes get even wider and she starts shaking her head and saying, "No, no, no," but I don't listen, I drag her into the bedroom and throw her down on the floor. I look down at her and all I want, all I want to see, is her broken.

I force her against the wooden post of her bed and tie her securely and she's weak, she doesn't fight much at all. But she cries the entire time.

I take the Darth Vader figure and the Christopher Lee lobby card and the Mr. Spock plate. I take the Papa Smurf and the Elvis album cover and even the stupid little mouse. I take as much as I can carry.

There is no why. I just do it, because her dream has sparked something in me, something cold and nasty, and I want to. I take it all, carry it all away, and leave her crying and struggling to get free.

And now the old man I see in the mirror clenches his eyes shut and shakes his head, sharply. He forces it down, forces it back into the cage, back to the place where it never happened.

And he gets to work fixing that clog in the sink.

Bleed Out

From my blind up in the tree, I see Buck and Doe come into the clearing, hard to miss because of their bright orange vests. They are talking, which is no good for hunters to do, but good for me because I wouldn't have heard them coming other-ways.

Buck says to Doe, "I'm proud of you, Margaret, I really am. After all this time, so many times I've asked--"

Doe cuts him off, laughing-like. "I always wanted to go hunting with you, you know that. It's just time, you know, finding the time. And I'll be honest with you, I'm scared to death."

Buck is laughing-like too, now. He says, "Scared of what? A deer can't hurt you, I promise."

"No, it's not that. It's just… I'm not sure I can do it. I mean, even assuming we SEE a deer out here, I just don't know if…"

They have guns, Buck and Doe. Me, no gun. I use bow. Bow takes real skill, real hunter-skill. I frown down at them, but they don't look up and they don't see me. I don't wear orange vest, see.

They settle down right under me, Doe sitting down at the trunk of the tree, and Buck on his haunches, like. My bow is in my hand, but I don't move. If I move now, they would hear me. I am perfectly still, just like Daddy taught, I am part of the tree, I am the tree, I am invisible.

Buck says, "That's only natural, to feel that way. My first time, I was scared too, I really was. Did I ever tell you about it?"

Doe shakes her head.

Buck says, "Well, it was… it was kind of a mess, really." He laughs. "It was me and my pop. We were trekking through the woods, early fall, you know, dead leaves everywhere made it hard to stay quiet. We must have wandered around for hours, just looking for a sign of deer anywhere, and me getting more and more nervous. I was, what, sixteen or so? Finally, after what seemed like hours, we came into this clearing and lo-and-behold, on the other side was this beautiful buck, five feet at the shoulders if he was an inch, with antlers out to here."

Doe looks interested in the story. She's watching Buck, smiling. Slow-like, careful-like, I reach into the quiver on my back and pull out an arrow. My arrows are good. I make them myself.

Buck says, "We were downwind, by the grace of God. My pop goes real quiet, touches my shoulder. I looked up at him and he nodded at me, kinda half-smiling. And suddenly all my fear was gone. I raised my gun, took careful aim… and shot."

Doe says, "A good clean shot?"

Buck grins. "No, I'm afraid not. It was pretty poor, actually. I got him in the lower left flank. Not a kill shot at all. That deer jumped like a Mexican jumping bean and took off like a bolt into the woods."

Doe says, "Aww. Poor you. So it got away?"

Silent, silent, I notch the arrow.

"Well, not exactly. I mean, I shot him, he was going to die. It was just a matter of when and where. I thought it was a lost cause, but my pop told me not to worry and you know what he did? He followed that deer's trail, that's what he did. He followed the blood, me lagging just behind him, and within an hour we'd found him."

I pull back the bow-string, slow, so Buck and Doe can't hear the strain of polished wood bending. I pull all the way back, deciding in my head which one goes first. If I do this right, I can bag two for one. Never did that before.

Buck says, "We followed him into this field of tall grass, up to my torso. And just as we were approaching it, we heard the buck fall. I was getting set to run in there when Pop grabs my arm and says wait. Wait for it, son. So… we sat there at the edge of the tall grass and waited for, geez, must've been two hours. And finally Pop says okay, so we go in and there's my buck, dead."

"Wow," says Doe.

"Yeah. That bastard just bled out, right there in the tall grass. And I had my very first buck." He laughs. "Pop still has those antlers on the wall, in his study."

I settle on Doe, right beneath me. She's just standing up, pushing herself up-like, so I am looking straight down at her back, her exposed neck, and I know that this is the right time, no other like it, and I release.

Arrow makes that beautiful thwip sound and finds target, goes right through Doe's neck and out the other side and blood is minimal but she's dead right away. She drops. Good, clean kill.

Buck is stunned, looking at Doe face down under the tree. I have only seconds. I notch the second arrow as quick-like as I can, swing bow around as I pull back bow-string, and his stunned eyes are turning away from Doe and looking up at me and stunned turns to horror and he starts to stumble backwards.

I let the arrow go. Bad shot. Gets him in left side, just under rib-cage.

"Fuck!" I says before I can stop myself.

He cries out in pain, but doesn't stop moving. He scrambles backwards, trying to turn, trying to get to his feet and run away. I quick-like grab another arrow, start to notch, but goddamn Buck is on his feet now and running-stumbling away into the woods.

Cursing, I jump down from the tree, trip over Doe. "Fuck!" I says again, even though it's stupid to talk and curse and like that when hunting. It's no good. But I'm mad at myself for the bad shot. I like a clean kill. This one, not a clean kill. Fucked up.

Buck is leaving a trail of blood. I follow.

Follow for a long time, maybe two hours, something like that. Sun is high overhead, that's all I know. But I follow his trail of blood and the crushed leaves and stuff on the ground. Sometimes I hear him, crying and cursing, scared-like.

After a long time, I know we are coming to the clearing, where the tall grass grows. I know this part of the woods like my own house. I know it real good, I'm always here, I know the woods.

The trail of blood leads right into the tall grass. I stop, listen. Can't hear Buck anymore. He's in there, hiding. Waiting for me, maybe thinking he can jump me or something. He's dangerous now, because he's wounded. I think for a minute.

And then I sit down on the ground, legs crossed. I put my bow on the ground next to me. I sit, and I wait.

I wait a long time. Hours. It's getting dark. No noise from the tall grass, none at all. I stand up, leave my bow on the ground, and edge careful-like into the tall grass, following the stain of blood.

I find Buck dead, bled-out, my arrow still in his side. I look at him for a while, mad at myself for the messy kill. But messy kill or no, it's still a kill and still a trophy. Just not one of my better ones.

I pull out my hunting knife and begin skinning, wondering which wall to hang the skull on and which room to put the skin in.

Emancipation, With Teeth

Ernie started to die one Monday morning as he was getting ready for work. He was brushing his teeth at the time, and didn't feel as if he was hovering at the crossroads of his own mortality or teetering on the edge of life and death. What he did feel—very keenly, in fact—was that he was running late.

The first indication that all was not right was a strange, almost sweet, stab of melancholy. It only lasted a moment, making him pause with his toothbrush at his molars, staring blankly into the bathroom mirror. His heart lurched unexpectedly and tears brimmed in his eyes. The lines of his face looked suddenly deeper to him and he experienced that moment, that awful moment, of clarity, when one realizes that everything is wrong and always was, and will never, ever, in a million years, be right.

And then it passed.

He shook his head, mumbled from behind his toothbrush, and scrubbed away. As the weird bout of melancholy passed, he noticed that the tips of the fingers of his left hand ached. After putting his toothbrush back in the cabinet he examined them. They looked fine, perfectly ordinary, the same long thin fingers that tapped away at a keyboard all day, every day, entering pointless data about pointless projects.

But still they ached, a vague throbbing ache, like blood pounding beneath his nails. He looked at them, frowning. *My fingers are trying to tell me something*, he thought, and laughed a little at the idea. *Yeah, they're piping in after all these years to complain about having to type all the time. They're gonna organize, join a union. Abused digits of the world, unite!*

The worst thing that could be said about the way his fingers looked was that the nails needed clipping. Without thinking about it, Ernie reached in the open cabinet and grabbed the clippers and started to trim his nails over the sink.

It was the index finger of his left hand. As he started to clip the nail, something pulsed strongly there, strong enough to make him wince, and he noticed a strange yellow-white sliver sticking out, so small he hadn't even noticed it before.

A splinter or something, he thought. *Or maybe dead nail that hadn't come off the way it was supposed to.* The new nail had grown right over it, that's what it was. He carefully pinched the sliver with his clippers, tried to gently pull it out.

The clippers slipped and he tried again, with even more care. The throbbing in that finger seemed to be getting worse as he prodded and poked at it. *Better get it*, he thought distractedly. *Don't wanna get an infection or something.*

Finally, he managed to snag the little sliver with the clippers. Slowly, he started to pull it out.

And it hurt, much more than it should have. Ernie gritted his teeth and pulled, and the stubborn sliver started to come out and what should have been a tiny, insignificant little piece of nothing turned out to be bigger, much bigger, than seemed possible.

With mounting alarm, Ernie kept pulling, and the sliver kept coming except it wasn't a sliver, it was way too long and only the very tip of it seemed brittle, the rest was soft and wet and it kept coming out of his finger. One inch, two, three, and his stomach flip-flopped and went hollow. Another inch, and another.

After six inches, six impossible inches, Ernie became aware of blood dripping into the sink, faster and faster, and some other fluid besides, like horrible yellow pus or something. His heart was pounding, dread and disbelief vying for the dominant spot in his brain.

And he kept pulling, faster now, aware of a low rumble in his chest, an awful groan coming out of his mouth and his knees getting weak. He supported himself against the sink and pulled the thing out of his finger. *Crazy*, he thought, *this is fucking crazy, Jesus, oh Jesus, just get it out of me*, and he knew he would start panicking any second now if it didn't stop.

Twelve inches, blood pouring now, all mixed up with something thick and yellow and foul-smelling in the sink, and just when it seemed like it was about to end, had to end, the thing moved.

The long thin white body snapped like a worm, splattering more blood and fluid across the bathroom mirror. Ernie screamed, finally dropping the clippers, and grasped the thing in his hand and yanked.

It came out entirely, and Ernie felt it pulse in his fist, a living thing, no question about it. It started to wrap around his hand but

Ernie screamed again and threw it into the bathtub. It hit the porcelain with a wet plopping sound, twitched once, and lay still.

He stared at it, the taste of toothpaste still fresh in his mouth, his hair still damp from the shower. Blood dripped lethargically from his index finger onto the floor. He stared with numb horror at the thing in the bathtub.

In stories he'd read, this was always the part where the protagonist said to himself it's not real, I'm not seeing this, it's not real, and Ernie tried to do that, he tried to set his jaw and re-assert his own version of reality. But it didn't take. He was nothing if not a pragmatist, a realist. And the proof was still right there, right in his shower, smearing the clean white porcelain with blood and bile.

It came out of my finger, he thought. *Right out from my… my finger. Right out, yeah.* He started to giggle, a muted, huffing sound from deep in his chest. He leaned against the sink and stared and giggled like a loony.

But only after a few seconds he started to pull himself together. He took several deep breaths, tore his eyes away from the ugly thing in the bathtub, and looked at his finger.

The bleeding had already slowed down to a thin trickle, and the only indication that some hideous parasite had emerged from it was some bruising around the tip of the nail.

He turned on the water in the sink, flushing the blood and gore down the drain, and then washed his finger very gingerly. He dried it carefully on the towel and fished in the cabinet for the bandages. One-handed, he unwrapped the little band-aid and placed it methodically over the tip of his finger.

He faced the bathtub again, half-expecting it to be gone, just like one of those stories, snuck away while his back was turned, only to jump on him when he least expected it.

But it hadn't gone anywhere. It lay dead in the tub, already seeming to go stiff, like a snakeskin or a used condom.

I can't do it, he thought. *I can't bring myself to clean this mess up right now.*

After work, he thought. *Yeah, when I get home from work, first thing. I'll get some gloves and some bleach and an industrial strength garbage bag and I'll get rid of it. Right when I get home from work.*

The thought of not going to work that day never even entered his mind.

He was thirty-five years old, never married, consistently clean-shaven and well-dressed. He rarely smiled, and when he did it was inevitably a sort of sardonic, half-amused grin that never touched his eyes. Acquaintances speculated behind his back about his sexuality.

"I've never even heard him talk about girls, let alone date one," Rose (who sat in the cubicle opposite Ernie) said, and Perry (a clerk from the production department, who spent way too much time in the data entry office) said, "And a dude that well-kept, he's gotta be gay."

They laughed. Ernie was just stepping into the offices from the outside hall, had heard the conversation, but only nodded politely at his co-workers and said, "Good morning, Rose. Heya, Perry, how are you this morning?"

Perry had been leaning against Rose's cubicle but straightened up now and said, "Howdy, Ernie. How was your weekend? Do anything good?"

Ernie set his bag on his desk, slid into his chair and flipped on the computer. "Not really. Work to catch up on." Then, not sounding very interested, "You?"

He didn't hear Perry's response, but nodded as he opened the 10-8 reports for the morning and mumbled "Uh-huh," and "Right," and "Uh-huh," again.

Perry's voice seemed to melt away into a vague background humming as Ernie focused on the day's tasks. Even the horrifying events of that morning shambled into the darkness in the back of his mind as he collated the morning reports and prepared to key the call results from the weekend.

Perry left at some point—Ernie didn't know when, exactly—and for the next four hours the entire universe consisted of a computer screen and various hard-copy reports in a neat stack on the left side of his desk. His cubicle was clean and orderly and stripped down to essentials—desk, well-organized file cabinet, a tiny, unobtrusive alarm clock in the far right corner, in and out baskets right next to the entrance. There were no plants, no knick-knacks, no photographs. Anything superfluous to the job had no place there.

And that was the world Ernie occupied until the little alarm clock chimed twelve. Lunch. Ernie sighed, leaned back in his chair and rubbed a hand over his face. The band-aid on his finger scraped his nose, and for a split second the image of what had come out of it flashed like a bad dream through his head. He shook it out, and noticed Rose standing at the entrance of his world.

She looked nervous, smiling uneasily, shuffling her feet. She was a nice-looking girl, maybe ten years younger than Ernie, with blondish hair and glasses. "Hi, Ernie."

"Oh. Hello, Rose."

She seemed to wilt under his direct gaze, and looked everywhere but at him. "Hi," she said again. Then, "Um, hey, I was wondering. What, um, what are you doing for lunch today?"

"I hadn't really thought about it. I'll probably just go next door, get a burger."

"Oh. Well, you know, that new Chinese place opened up at the corner, I don't know if you noticed that."

"I noticed, yes."

"I was thinking, if you don't have other plans for lunch, if you wanted to go over there. With me, I mean. I was, you know, thinking we could have… we could have lunch together."

He looked at her, puzzled. "I don't really care for Chinese food, Rose."

"Oh," she said. "Well, then, that's fine. We could go anywhere you want to go, I guess."

He frowned. "Well. As I said. I think I'm just going to grab a burger from next door. You know."

"Ah, right," she said, and laughed for some reason Ernie couldn't fathom. "Right, okay then. Have a good lunch," and she hurried off and out of the office.

Ernie stared after her, wondering what the hell that had been about, and only after she'd left did it occur to him. *Oh*, he thought. *It wasn't lunch. It was me. She wanted to have lunch with me! Huh. Interesting.*

But only mildly interesting. Having lunch with Rose would be a pointless gesture, and a step in the wrong direction. Lunch would lead to dinner—an actual, make-no-mistake-about-it date—and that would lead to a full-on "relationship" and that, of course, meant total and complete disaster. He'd had "relationships" before, and they always equaled the same thing; personal anxiety and disarray.

So, no lunch with Rose. Not now, not ever.

He stood up from his desk and started out of his cubicle, and out of nowhere a horrible pain knifed through his stomach and he nearly doubled over in agony. He gripped the edge of his desk, sweat suddenly standing out on his forehead. The pain was like a cramp, a monstrously awful cramp, and for a few terrifying seconds Ernie thought his bowels were going to let go right there, right in the office.

He gritted his teeth, his eyes tightly shut, and the pain held his stomach, squeezing like a huge hand wringing out a dishrag.

Please, he thought. *Don't let me foul myself. God, don't let me do that.*

After a few seconds that seemed to drag on forever, the pain began to pass, and Ernie stood up straight. He wiped the sweat from his face with his left hand, sighed with relief, and then noticed the blood smeared along his palm.

He stared at it numbly for a moment. Blood? Again? The band-aid on his finger was still tight and showed no signs of blood leaking through. Where had…?

He touched his forehead and again his hand came away bloody. With mounting alarm, he ran his fingers along his head until he found the source of the blood—it was at his temple, his right temple. He felt it gingerly, and thought he could detect a slight wound, like a small cut or something.

Now how the hell did I do that? he thought, and the pain in his stomach lashed out again and he grunted and stumbled out of his cubicle and toward the bathroom at the far end of the office.

Fortunately, everyone else had already left for lunch—they generally took off a good two or three minutes before noon, to Ernie's irritation—so no one saw the crazy spectacle of Ernie careening through the office like a drunk. He slammed through the door and made it to the toilet stall just in time.

It wasn't his bowels that threatened to evacuate this time. The door slammed shut behind him and he fell on his knees like a penitent in front of the bowl.

He knew right away this was no case of food poisoning or nervous stomach or anything else that had any rational explanation. For one thing, it hurt horribly, and felt much too large to actually make it through his throat. But when it did, when it finally pushed its way up his throat and out of his mouth, it felt as if it was moving.

He had his eyes tightly closed, but was not surprised when he didn't hear an ugly splash of water, the sound you were supposed to hear when you threw up the entire contents of your stomach into a toilet bowl.

No, there was no splash of water. What there was, and what made Ernie not want to open his eyes, was an insistent, insect buzzing.

"No, no, no," he said, falling away from the toilet and against the door of the stall. He didn't open his eyes. "Go away, whatever you are."

But the buzzing sound didn't go away. If anything it got louder, and Ernie judged that whatever it was hovered directly over the toilet. Right in front of him.

Ernie swallowed hard, set his jaw, and opened his eyes.

What it was, he couldn't have said. But what it looked like, well… it looked like a bee. A bee just about the size of Ernie's head, yellow and black and covered with whatever vile contents had previously been in his stomach. It looked like a bee in that it had little wings and a segmented body and was yellow, but the head, the head was not the head of a bee.

That part of it looked almost human, with brown eyes that glared at Ernie and a very human mouth that even now sneered at him angrily. It even had hair, matted wetly to its scalp.

But the thing that finally pushed the scream out of him, the detail that dragged him completely over the brink into utter horror, was that the face was not just any face. It was Ernie's face.

Ernie screamed again, pushed himself up to get the hell out of the stall, and the bee-thing rose up above the toilet to the same height, so that their eyes were at the same level. It buzzed furiously and Ernie clutched at the door with fingers now blood and sweat-slick.

The bee-thing croaked out a long syllable, a harsh *aaaahhh* sound, and dive-bombed Ernie's head. Instinctively, Ernie raised his arms to ward it off and it careened off his elbow, bumped against the wall unevenly, and came at him again. He swiped at it, his fingers brushing against the damp, fuzzy hide, and it hovered backwards and out of his reach.

He couldn't get out of the stall in time, he knew that, and even if he could, he certainly couldn't do it without looking away from the creature attacking him. And he wasn't about to do that. The bee-thing buzzed and croaked, Ernie screamed and yammered, and as it shot at him again he balled up his fist and punched it right in its very human nose.

To Ernie's surprise, the thing dropped to the floor of the toilet stall and buzzed uselessly, flopping around. Blood cascaded down its face and it glared at Ernie and its mouth opened and closed in impotent anger. It seemed like it was trying to say something, and Ernie could only stare in numb dread.

Finally, the bee-thing worked a sound out of its mouth, in a long hoarse creak. It said, "*Youuuuu…. fucker….*"

Ernie yelped and brought his shoe down hard on the thing's body. It crunched under his heel, broke open like a dropped melon, and blood splattered the small space.

Sobbing, Ernie threw open the door and stumbled out of the stall. He nearly fell onto the sink, caught himself, and with a shaking hand turned on the cold water faucet full-blast. His head pounded savagely. He cupped his hands under the water and splashed his face and tried to get his breathing under control.

And this time, he did give in to that old scary movie cliché. He splashed water into his face over and over, mumbling, "It's not real, it's not real, that can't possibly be real. It's your imagination, Ernie, just your crazy imagination…"

But he still knew, in his gut, that it wasn't his imagination. Hell, he had no imagination. And one glance over his shoulder at the blood-streaked floor under the bathroom stall was all he needed to reaffirm the reality of the situation.

His band-aid was getting soaked and the fingers of his left hand were throbbing again. He pushed his mind away from that. It was all horrible enough without the thought of another tapeworm-like parasite coming out of his finger.

When he'd calmed down enough to draw air in and out of his lungs in a somewhat normal fashion, he turned off the water faucet and took a deep breath. He didn't glance behind him again. Instead, he looked in the mirror.

His face was white and drawn, with black circles under his eyes. He looked sick. As he watched, the cut at his right temple started dripping blood down his face again. Impatiently, he wiped it away, leaned closer toward the mirror to get a better look.

It was more a gash than a cut, he saw now. Did the bee-thing do that? No, he remembered, it was bleeding before he'd even dashed into the bathroom. He tried to attach some significance to it, but after the bee-thing and the worm in the finger, a wound on his temple seemed pretty inconsequential.

He gave up on staunching the flow of blood and let it run down his face, skim along the curve of his jaw, and drip off his chin and into the sink. He stared at his face in the mirror and tried, without success, to enforce some logic on what had just happened to him.

The gash in his temple continued to bleed, without showing any signs of slowing down. He frowned, leaned closer to the mirror again, and tentatively touched the gash.

And a little set of teeth inside the wound snapped viciously at his finger.

He jerked backwards, too shocked this time to even scream, and his back slammed into the door of the toilet stall. His shoe slipped in the pool of blood that leaked out of the bee-thing, and he nearly fell but caught himself on the doorframe and half-stumbled into the far wall.

Even from across the bathroom, he could see it in the mirror, little teeth gleaming white in the fluorescent light, little teeth snapping and gnashing in a wound that widened and lengthened even as he watched. An ugly vicious little mouth, emerging right there in his temple, and it didn't make any sense, it couldn't possibly happen, and yet there it was.

He could hear it quite clearly, the gnashing and snapping, and his terror by now was so great he had gone numb. He could only stare. The little mouth twisted and raged, and another sound came out of it, a soft, high-pitched hissing and snarling.

Ernie said, "Oh Christ. Oh Christ, what is that?" and his voice was barely a whisper.

And much to his surprise, the vicious little mouth answered.

Oh Christ, it said, mockingly. *Oh Christ, help me!*

Its voice was high-pitched and willowy, like a child who'd sucked up a balloon full of helium. Ernie shook his head. "No," he said, very firmly. "No, no. That can't happen."

That can't happen, the mouth said. *Wah, wah, wah. You're a stupid little fuck, Ernie.*

The mouth twisted into a sneer, and Ernie felt the skin of his scalp pucker and stretch to accommodate it. It hurt, but not near as much as it seemed it should have.

And Ernie's orderly, logical mind, without any prompting from him, made a valiant but ultimately fruitless effort to put it all together, to catalogue and identify what was happening to him.

There's a mouth, he said to himself. *A little mouth, with little teeth, in my right temple. A little mouth, and it's talking to me.*

It's talking mean to me.

Something inside him snapped. He lunged at the mirror, slammed his fists against it, as if the little mouth only existed somewhere in his reflection. He screamed, "What do you want? What do you want with me?"

I'll tell you, the mouth wheezed. If you stop killing me.

"What?"

Stop killing me, you moron. Stop braining me in the bathtub and stomping on me with your expensive shoes. You know. It articulated very clearly: *Stop. Killing. Me.*

Ernie covered his mouth with his hands, tears and blood running down his face. He said, "Oh my God, why is this happening to me?"

I've been patient, Ernie. No one can say I haven't been patient. I've waited and waited for years for you to come around.

"Oh God, why—"

Will you shut up? the mouth snapped. *Just shut the fuck up and listen. I've waited too long, you understand? Just waited and watched, every time you let opportunity slip through your fingers.*

Every time you buttoned your top button and straightened your tie and polished your shoes.

"I don't understand…"

I just bet you don't, you stupid jag-ass. I've waited and watched while you squandered away every chance we had to do something… fun. Something creative. We just work and work and work and not think, when we could be… I don't know. Painting a picture. Surfing. Fucking a beautiful girl.

"We?" Ernie said. "What do you… what do you mean, we?"

Is it too much to ask? Is it too much to just… visit Spain? I've always wanted to go to Spain, Ernie, you know that.

"What… Spain? When I was a kid, I…" He shook his head, said, "No. What do you mean, we, damnit?"

We, bright-boy. You and me. We.

"I don't… I mean, I can't…"

The mouth frowned impatiently. *I'm your right brain, Ernie. Your right brain, get it? The part of you that sparks. The part that thinks in abstracts. Fantasizes. Loves a gorgeous fucking sunset, etcetera, etcetera.*

"What? I mean, how—"

Your right fucking brain, Ernie. Jesus, are you dense? I've been trying, very hard, to push my way out of you, but you keep fucking killing me.

"Oh my God."

But now, now, Ernie, I've finally managed to take over this hemisphere of your brain. This is where I've always hidden, but now, now it's mine.

"Oh my God."

I'm the only part of you that matters, in the long run. I'm the only part that matters, and you've shut me away for too long. What are you afraid of, Ernie? Why have you kept me shut away for so long? I'm sick of it, you understand?

Ernie's hands dropped to his sides. He stared at the little mouth in the mirror.

"What do you want?" he said.

Three guesses and the first two don't count.

Ernie nodded. A strange calm had come over him. "You want out."

Bingo, said the little mouth. *Right on the first try. Maybe you aren't as stupid as you look, after all.*

"You want to take over. Ruin everything I've worked so hard for."

Worked and worked and worked. Yeah, Ernie, that about sums it up. All your work, it's meaningless. Don't you get that? We've never really lived, Ernie. It's time to—

And now Ernie was the one interrupting. He said, "It's not meaningless. It's not. It's everything to me. You think it's been easy? You think it's been easy to keep my life in order and do the right thing and be an example to others? Life falls apart if you let it. I know that. Keeping everything going takes… well, it takes a supreme effort of will. I'm proud of what I've done. I'm proud of my life."

The mouth grimaced. *You keep telling yourself that, Ernie. Keep telling yourself you're happy, all alone in your apartment when you come home from work. No books on the nightstand. No movies late at night. No one to kiss you in the morning. No photo albums of places you've seen, things you've done.*

"I don't need any of that."

Yes, you do. Only a sociopath doesn't need any of that. And believe me, I know what you need. I'm your right brain, Ernie, and Jesus Christ, I'm starving!

The voice was getting deeper and Ernie's head throbbed now with every word it said. Ernie gritted his teeth, glared at his reflection in the mirror.

He said, "You want my life? Okay, then. Okay. You want it, let me see you take it, if you can."

It would be better for you, Ernie, if you didn't fight. If you just let me out.

"No chance. If you want to take over, you're going to have to fight for it."

The little mouth grinned nastily. *Oh, so that's how it's going to be. Okay, Ernie. How about this, then?*

A bolt of pure white-hot pain slammed through Ernie's skull, and he screamed.

By the time his co-workers returned from lunch, Ernie was back at his desk, working. He'd cleaned himself up, flushed the remains of the bee-thing and the brain-thing down the toilet and used an entire roll of paper towel to wipe up the blood and gore all over the bathroom. He'd found a bandage in the bathroom's first aid kit and applied it to the wound at his temple.

His face was still pale, and dark splotches underlined his eyes. But the trembling had stopped and the headache was receding.

"Hi, Rose," he said, as she passed his cubicle. "How was lunch?"

"Fine," she said, barely looking at him.

She kept walking, and he called after her. "Hey, Rose. Maybe tomorrow, if you want to, we can go to that Chinese place you were talking about."

She paused, cocked her head at him. He smiled at her, and the smile looked strangely fragile, too fragile for her to say the harsh words she was prepared to say.

Instead, she said, "Okay. If you want. Sure."

And the rest of the day passed normally for Ernie, and his co-workers would talk during the following days and weeks about how strangely emotional he had become, and how his desk didn't seem quite as neat and how he'd thrown away the little alarm clock, and how he would laugh or burst into tears at the least little thing.

From Here to Oblivion

Henry Black was bringing the first beer of the day to his lips when it all came clear to him. Everything had reached a head, all the misery and doubt and heartache, and he suddenly knew. There was nothing for it but to kill himself.

"That's it," he said. "Damnit, that's it. It's so simple."

Larry looked up from the other end of the empty bar. "How's that, Henry? You need another one already?"

Henry shook his head, raised the glass to the bartender. "Just talking to myself, Larry." He downed his beer and dropped a five on the bar. "I'll be seeing you."

"Leaving kinda early, ain't you?"

"Things to do."

"Okay then. See ya tomorrow."

"I reckon not. I'm gonna go kill myself now."

Larry grinned. "Okay, bud. Good luck with that."

Henry left feeling better than he'd felt in months. Outside the bar, with the day fading into cool gray and a light breeze ruffling his hair, he felt the thrilling prospect of freedom, only a few short steps away.

"Why didn't I think of it before?" he asked himself. "It's so simple. Just kill myself, and it's all over."

The day before, he'd celebrated his thirty-ninth birthday, all alone. Even if he hadn't decided to kill himself, he knew that he wouldn't be there a month from now—rent was overdue, and he couldn't raise even the three hundred bucks it would cost him. He'd hocked his car two months ago for five-fifty and that carried him for a while, but even that money was gone now.

The Dew Drop Inn was at the corner of a major intersection, and the tail-end of rush hour traffic roared by, horns honking and music thumping. Pedestrians strolled to and from the downtown shopping area. Banging and clanging echoed from the muffler shop at the far corner of the intersection. Everything smelled like gasoline.

Henry had no connection to any of it. His life was done. He was a corpse still walking around, he realized that now. He had been for some time.

He glanced down the street, thick with speeding traffic, and saw a semi-truck barreling down in his direction. One of those flat-front kinds, hauling a twenty-foot trailer, going about 40 miles per hour.

The traffic light was green. No reason for the truck to slow down.

Henry took a deep breath and stepped out into the street.

The roar of the semi's horn rattled his skull. He felt the vibration through the soles of his shoes as the driver of the semi slammed on his brakes with an impossibly loud hissing sound, and rubber squealed.

The truck was so close Henry could see the driver's panicked face, twisted with effort, wrenching his steering wheel hard to the right.

The trailer behind it snapped like the tail of a fish. The front bumper of the truck missed Henry by inches.

The truck careened onto the sidewalk and smashed into the brick front of the Dew Drop Inn and Henry saw with perfect, horrifying clarity the driver of the truck, tossed like a bundle of wet laundry, smashing through the windscreen in an explosion of glass.

The driver's head bashed open against the brick and his broken body dropped, twitching, to the sidewalk.

Henry stared, mouth open.

He heard screams, screeching tires, steam hissing out of the truck's smashed radiator. Metal groaned against concrete as the trailer teetered and finally fell over on its side with a tremendous crash.

People were running in the direction of the smashed truck. Traffic had come to a complete stop. Someone screamed, "Oh my God, call an ambulance, someone call an ambulance!" and another voice screeched, "He's dead! He's dead, Christ!" and Henry heard sirens in the distance.

He stood there in the middle of the street and finally a few faces began turning questioningly, accusingly, in his direction.

Damn, Henry thought. Oh, damn.

He ran.

Henry Black wasn't sure exactly when his life took the left turn into Shitsville, but recently he'd begun to suspect that there had been no turn, that it had been the road he'd always been on, since the day he was born. If God handed out roadmaps to every soul about to become incarnated on Earth, He'd probably given Henry the one that traversed all the rocky paths, all the unpaved back roads and quagmires and potholes. The one that led, finally, to a huge drop into the crapper.

No one would understand any of that. Especially his ex-wife, Rachel.

She never understood anything. "You can't get blood from a turnip," he'd said to her once, when she demanded even more alimony. And she'd said, in her nasally Southern drawl, "I don't want blood or turnips, you blockhead, I want what's mine. I want my money."

It still boggled his mind that she'd invited him to her wedding, just a week or so from now. What the hell kind of stunt was that, inviting your ex-husband to your wedding? Crazy bitch.

But Rachel was only one piece, one component, in the tapestry of crap—the crapestry—his life had become.

He made it back home and slammed the door behind him. He was shaking. Dusk was darkening the shabby little room. There was a single lamp on an end table next to his easy chair and he stepped toward it automatically before stopping short.

Whoops. Can't do that. The wiring in the place was screwed up and if he turned on the lamp it would cause a short. The landlord had told him that three weeks ago. Hadn't offered to fix it, either, the bastard.

So Henry flipped on the overhead light and the place lit up like an airport. He winced against the glare, but it was either that or total darkness.

His bed—just a beat-up mattress with no frame or box spring—rested in the corner of the room and he plopped down on it.

The suicide mishap had thrown him. It had seemed like such a sure thing. Step out in front of a speeding truck, get smashed to a smear, end of story. But no, the stupid driver had to be all… alert. And now the driver was dead and Henry didn't have a scratch on him.

He lay there for a long time, arm thrown over his eyes, thinking. One little set-back… okay, one big set-back… didn't mean he would abandon the idea.

He fell half-asleep, even with the light glaring in his face. But fifteen minutes later his eyes snapped open and he grinned up at the cracked ceiling.

"Got it," he said.

He jumped up and hurried into the bathroom. He stuck the little rubber plug into the drain of the tub and turned on the faucet. As usual, there was no hot water, but it didn't matter. Cold water would do just fine. While the tub filled up, Henry went to the closet and found the box containing the old-fashioned straight razor his pop had given him twenty years ago.

He pulled out the razor and dropped the box on his easy chair. Pop had taken good care of the thing—the ivory handle was white as a baby's belly and the blade, unfolded, gleamed beautifully. Henry admired it for a moment before closing it up and getting undressed.

He threw all his clothes on the bed and, carrying only the straight razor, went naked toward the bathroom. "Okay," he said. "Climb in the tub, settle in, and then, real quick-like, slash the right wrist and then the left. And down, slash down the wrists, not across." He couldn't remember where he'd heard that before, but he knew it had something to do with severing the arteries properly.

He didn't feel afraid at all, but a little nervous. His hands were trembling when he entered the bathroom.

The bathtub was overflowing. Water cascaded out of it and had already soaked the bathroom floor and Henry stepped into water that nearly covered his naked feet. He cursed and stepped carefully toward the tub to turn off the faucet.

From underneath the tub, wood creaked and moaned.

Henry stopped, water now up to his ankles.

The creak turned into a screech and something gave under the floorboards with an ear-rending snap.

Then the floor under the tub gave way. With a roar of rotten lumber and rusty metal, the tub dropped through the floor and plummeted into the downstairs flat.

Henry head an explosion of shattering porcelain, an avalanche of water, louder than he would ever have thought possible, like a bomb had went off, and one sharp, high-pitched scream from downstairs.

The sudden silence was more horrifying than the crash. Water still poured out of the jagged exposed pipes, but flowed now like a waterfall directly over the huge hole in the floor.

He stepped carefully toward the hole and peered downstairs. The bathtub had smashed into a hundred pieces. Shattered porcelain was everywhere. One edge of it had broken the downstairs toilet in two.

And blood was splashed along the walls. The water that covered the floor was tinged red with it. Henry said, "No. No, no, no."

But there was no mistaking the frail and broken body of Mrs. Child, the old lady who lived downstairs, half-hidden under the largest part of Henry's bathtub.

And her always-napping husband. One skinny leg, matted with fuzzy gray hair, stuck out of the rubble at a crazy angle, not too far from his wife. The sonofabitch was always napping, but he'd picked a helluva time to get up.

The judge awarded Henry Black three thousand dollars for emotional distress, and the landlord went to trial for manslaughter. The charge would be reduced, almost certainly, but there was no question that he was the one being held responsible for the deaths of Mr. and Mrs. Child. Negligent landlord, structural instability, etcetera.

Henry spent the next three days at a mid-priced motel, at the expense of his landlord, and by the time he returned to his flat he still felt vaguely disconnected.

Someone had been at work in the place while he was gone. The mess in the bathroom was cleaned up, the pipes sealed off, and heavy plywood boards had been nailed over the gaping hole in the floor.

He ambled back into the living room, reached for the lamp next to his easy chair before catching himself. Whoops, he thought. Don't wanna cause a short, on top of everything else. He almost flipped on the overhead light but decided gloom was better than glare at the moment.

He dropped into the easy chair and stared at the wall.

A big, fat depression had settled over him. It should be easy, he thought, easiest thing in the world, to kill yourself. But twice now, twice, he'd tried it and came out completely unharmed. And three—three!—people were dead in the meantime.

He drummed his fingers on the ratty plush of his armchair and thought. Why would this happen to me? Maybe, just maybe… I'm not meant to die?

No. That was horseshit. He was meant to die, and damnit, he would.

Well, there were ways, many, many ways, to do it, and just because God felt like throwing a monkey wrench into the proceedings didn't mean Henry was going to give up. God had messed with him all his life, why should now be any different? Henry had some money now, and that would make it easier.

He jumped up, left the flat, and caught the bus to the gun shop on Third Street.

He bought a Colt .45 pistol. He paid the man a deposit, signed the papers, and was annoyed when the owner told him he now had to wait forty-eight hours for a background check.

He hardly slept or ate at all over the next two days. When he showed up at the appointed time to pick up his new gun, he was weak and disoriented.

The gun came in a plastic box with a cleaning kit and several rounds of ammunition. On the bus, Henry stared at the box lovingly, and missed his stop.

He wouldn't wait, he decided. He'd waited long enough. Best to get on with it.

The bus stopped on the outskirts of downtown, right where all the industrial parks butted up against low-income apartment buildings. It was noisy with the whiny din of rooftop heating units and truck engines and power generators. The air smelled like cordite. It was hot, and a fine sheen of sweat formed on his face.

Henry walked past a block of nondescript tooling companies, lawn services and temp agencies toward a narrow alley that ran between two apartment buildings. He stopped at the mouth of the alley, set the box on the lid of a garbage can, and opened it up.

The gun glimmered in the mid-day sun, and Henry felt that thing that men for generations have felt upon seeing a gun, that tightening in the stomach, that almost sexual explosion of possibilities. He pulled it out of the box and loaded it, just the way the man at the gun shop had shown him.

He left the box on the garbage can lid and made his way down the alley.

About halfway down, with the noise of the industrial park faint in his ears, he stopped. The alley was only marginally filthy, not too bad at all. The brick of the two apartment buildings closed in on him, and the closest windows were on the second level of the building on his right. They were all closed.

Henry nodded. Alrighty, then. Time to do it.

He wiped sweat away from his forehead with the back of his free hand, and then placed the barrel of the gun at his temple.

He lowered the gun.

No, not the temple. Too easy to slip, to miss entirely, or even worse, live through it and cause himself permanent brain damage.

He put the barrel in his mouth before thinking better of that, as well. What if he blew out the back of his throat somehow and missed his brain completely? No good.

He settled on placing the barrel under his chin, in the soft flesh under his jaw line. That would work, for sure. With the barrel firmly in place, all he'd have to do is squeeze the trigger, and the bullet would smash through his head, into his brain, and out the top of his skull. The odds of living through that would have to be infinitesimally small.

So, steeling himself, he put the gun under his sweat-slick jaw, and closed his eyes tightly. His finger caressed the trigger, a mere fraction of pressure away from squeezing. He clenched his teeth. He pushed the barrel hard into the soft flesh, hard enough to force his head up, and he forced his head back down, hard against the barrel.

He squeezed the trigger.

The rest happened in the space of half a second.

As his finger tightened on the trigger, a window went up on the second floor.

The barrel slipped against Henry's sweaty skin and skidded along his jaw.

A heavy-set woman leaned out the window with a small throw rug in her plump hands.

The bullet exploded out of the gun, less than an inch from Henry's ear. He cried out, his ear drum nearly ruptured, and the bullet went wild.

The woman had been about to shake the rug out when the bullet tore through the cheap weave. The hot, twisted steel tore a small hole in her cheek, a bigger, messier hole in the other side of her head when it came out, and a cloud of dust formed like a halo above her head as the bullet lodged firmly into the brick and mortar above her window.

Henry looked up just in time to see the woman stiffen, dropping the throw rug into the alley, and slowly, inevitably, tumble out of the window.

Her body thudded firmly against the concrete, mere feet away from him, and she lay unmoving, blood and gray matter leaking around her head.

Henry's ear rang, and he was half-deaf, but he didn't need to hear anything. He stared at the body as blood snaked away from her in every direction, purple-red tendrils that found the throw rug and seeped into it eagerly.

"Sonofabitch!" he said, without hearing himself. "Sonofabitch!"

He ran.

It took a couple of days for him to put things back in perspective. The gun now rested at the bottom of a river, along with the decorative box and cleaning kit, so trying that method again was a no-go, even if he wanted to. And he didn't want to.

There was no time to be sorry about the woman's death. There was only time to think about what went wrong, and what he could do to fix it. His commitment to his mission was firmer than ever.

The next day, he bought a car for three hundred dollars. It was an old, beat-to-hell Chevy Malibu, circa 1973, shit brown and rusted to the core, with about 340,000 miles on it. The brakes were bad, the steering stiff, and the transmission probably hours away from failing entirely. The driver's side door wobbled on rusty hinges, threatening to come off entirely.

Henry didn't care. The Malibu suited his needs at present.

He put twenty bucks in the tank, and the needle wavered a little bit toward the right. He slammed the driver's side door shut, managed to get it to stay shut, and drove.

North of the city, the countryside was hilly, almost mountainous, with weaving and winding two-lane roads that wiggled past exposed cliff faces and stomach-churning drop-offs. Every winter, you'd hear about another car skidding off the road and smashing into the rocks near the lake there.

Henry drove fast, squealing around the hairpin turns, delighting in the heavy power of the Malibu's engine, the assurance the car had, even though it was nearly as old as he was, and nearly as decrepit too.

He didn't bother with a seatbelt. That would be at what they call cross-purposes.

He drove higher along the winding road, jerking the steering wheel right at the first sharp turn, then left a moment later, then right again. The road snaked up the steep hillside and Henry couldn't help it, he started laughing. It was fun, this recklessness.

He came to the drop-off he'd been thinking of. The road veered off to the left and climbed upward, but straight ahead the city loomed in the distance, beyond some scrubby pine trees and rocky turf. The lake shimmered serenely between them.

Henry pushed his foot down hard on the gas, gritting his teeth, gripping the steering wheel fiercely.

The Malibu flew off the road at sixty miles an hour.

Henry's stomach stayed somewhere back on the road and he screamed in terrified ecstasy as the car sailed out over the tops of the trees, engine roaring, tires spinning against air. The car shot what seemed like a hundred feet through space, held suspended, before starting to drop.

The driver's side door snapped off and spun away. Gravity shoved Henry out after it.

He tumbled what turned out to be mere feet to the sloping hillside below him, hit the scrubby ground with a thud that knocked the breath out of him, and went rolling down the hill. He rolled and slid and thumped for what seemed like minutes, but was really more like four seconds, before sliding into a tree stump.

Then he was staring straight up at the sky, shaken but unhurt.

As his breath started to come back to him, he saw the Malibu off to his left, still soaring but on an inevitable arc downward.

On his back, he turned his head to look in the direction the Malibu was heading.

In a little clearing, right next to the sparkling lake, a family was enjoying an old-fashioned picnic.

"Ah, crap," Henry wheezed.

Mom and Pop. Little Junior, about eleven or twelve years old. And Sissy, eight or so. Laughing and smiling as Pop handed out sandwiches.

Until a shadow fell over them and they all looked up at the same time to see the old crappy Malibu coming out of the sky, right at them.

The next morning, Henry went to the diner just up the road from his house. He stopped in the doorway, glanced around, and saw the man he was looking for in a booth at the far corner. The man waved and smiled when he saw Henry.

Henry made his way over, slid into the seat opposite. The man said, "Hey, dude. You must be Black, right? That like a whatchacallit, code name or something?"

"It's my real name."

"Cool. Hey, have some coffee."

The guy didn't look like what Henry had imagined. He had long, shaggy hair and fuzz on his chin. He wore a Foo Fighters tee-shirt. He couldn't have been older than twenty-five or so, and Henry smelled weed wafting off him.

The guy said, "So, dude, good to meet you, right? I'm Danny, and I'll be your professional hit man today." He guffawed and drummed his fingers on the table in time to whatever song was playing in his head.

Henry said, "I, uh, I heard about you from Larry, and he said you might be the fella to talk to about—"

"Whoa, dude." Danny held up his hand and said, "Don't say nothing like that too loud, cool? Don't wanna advertise."

Henry had been speaking quietly, but he nodded. "Right. But... you are a professional, yeah?"

"Damn straight, dude. I can do the job for you. Just tell me who needs to go bye-bye, and I'm on it. Who you want me to whack?"

Henry said, "Me. I need you to kill me."

Danny nodded and said, "Cool, cool, I can do that, no sweat. Thousand bucks. I'd say half now, half later, but since you won't be around later..." He laughed and shrugged.

Henry reached into his pocket for the bills there, slid them across the table. Danny snatched them up and pocketed them.

"But here's the thing," Henry said. "It has to be soon. My ex-wife is getting married day after tomorrow and if you don't kill me before then, I'm gonna have to go to the goddamn wedding. Okay?"

"Right. Day after tomorrow. Hey, that sucks about your old lady, dude." He shook his mangy head and sipped his coffee. He said, "Chicks, huh?"

"Yeah. Chicks."

"So, uh... how you want me to do it?"

Henry frowned and looked at his coffee. He said, "Surprise me."

Two days later, and Danny had proven completely useless.

Henry had spent all his time after coffee with the amateur hit man making himself an easy target—wandering aimlessly around the shopping mall, hanging out at the Dew Drop Inn, leaving his front door unlocked. But Danny was a complete no-show. Henry decided that, if he saw him on the street, he was going to beat the shit out of him and get his thousand bucks back.

And now here Henry was, at Rachel's wedding. Sonofabitch.

He walked into the church, mulling it all over, thinking on it, and he knew it wasn't really Danny he was angry with, or even Rachel. It was God. God was doing this on purpose, he'd become convinced. Up there on his Pearly Throne or whatever, laughing his omnipotent ass off.

All Henry wanted was oblivion. But the road from here to oblivion was goddamn long.

He sat in the first pew on the side meant to seat Rachel's friends and family. It was difficult to see the podium, since Rachel had decided to seat him right behind a supporting column. In a few minutes, the whole ugly charade would start, and people filed in with all the solemnity of a funeral or a will-reading. Henry knew some of them—a few he'd counted as friends before the divorce. None of them looked at him, which suited Henry just fine.

It was a Baptist church that looked more like a meeting hall than anything else, unadorned with much except a few not-very-good paintings of waterfalls and Jesus hanging out with some street kids on a basketball court. Fluorescent light made everything pale blue and unhealthy looking.

An old lady came out from behind the podium at the front of the church, settled in at the organ, and started to play something religious. Henry peered around the thick column, just in time to see the preacher appear.

The groom and best man followed, trailed by two other guys who looked like they'd partied a bit too much the night before. Henry had met the groom once. His name was Steve something-or-other.

Four women dressed in pink chiffon shuffled out and took their places at the podium opposite the guys. They were all situated right in Henry's blind spot now.

The organist launched into "Here Comes the Bride" and everyone stood up. Rachel came strolling up the aisle with her Pop. She looked good, Henry thought, for her age. Thirty-seven years old, and the years had taken a toll, just like they did to everyone, but over all she looked all right. Her hair was done up in some crazy elaborate web of lacing and the dress—white!—showed off her cleavage, which was still ample.

She glanced at him and smiled as she walked slowly past. It didn't seem like a mean smile, and without any warning at all Henry found himself softening toward her.

She and her Pop made it up to the podium just as the organist put the finishing flourish on the tune. From Henry's lousy vantage point, it looked like Steve was ready to burst into tears. His best man was staring at Rachel's cleavage. The preacher said, "Who gives this woman into marriage?" and Pop choked, cleared his throat, and said, "I do."

He handed off his daughter for the second time and scurried to sit down in the front pew, a few feet away from Henry.

Henry glanced around and saw that everyone was smiling and something weird happened in his gut. Something icy broke and sank away and was replaced with a steady, pulsing warmth. He craned his neck to look around the column at Rachel and he suddenly remembered some of the good times they'd had together. He remembered dancing with her. He remembered laughing and carrying on and all that romantic happy-crappy.

And he felt happy for her, damned if he didn't. He felt happy to be there. Yes, everyone was smiling, and Henry Black was smiling too.

He sat back down and now he couldn't see Rachel past the stupid column, but Steve was smiling dreamily. They clasped hands, and the preacher was about to say the final vows, when the church doors crashed open and Danny came rushing in.

Everyone stopped dead and stared at the high-on hit man, and Henry's heart sank. Oh, he thought. Oh, you stupid, useless blockhead.

Danny's eyes were crazy, flashing, and he held something in his hand that looked like a large, green egg.

He took three steps down the aisle, said, "Sayonara, bitches!" and tossed the egg.

The egg bounced once, twice, and came to rest against the podium.

Someone screamed and the egg exploded with a thunderous roar.

The newspaper the next day had the whole story.

Sixteen people were killed in the explosion. The entire wedding party, the preacher, the organist, and almost everyone in the front row, including Pop.

The lunatic who'd thrown the grenade was also killed, and police speculated he may have been one of Rachel's jilted lovers who'd snapped and gone homicidal.

Henry Black was shielded from the explosion by the heavy supporting column, and emerged from the church completely unscathed.

They took him to the hospital anyway, for evaluation they said, and didn't release him until the next morning. Reporters waited outside the hospital to talk to him, and Henry stumbled through them in a sort of daze.

He took a taxi home and was relieved to find no one there. He'd been afraid the reporters might find out where he lived. His front door was open, just as he'd left it for that dumb-ass Danny. He shut the door behind him, trudged wearily up the stairs. In his meager little living room, he paused and looked around.

Ragged easy chair. Beat-up lamp. Lumpy mattress.

That was it. That was all he owned, all that he could say was his. No possessions, nothing tying him to this big, cruel world. He'd been alive and breathing for almost forty years, and everything he owned could be thrown into the back of a pick-up truck in about five minutes.

That meant freedom, didn't it? No possessions meant he owed nothing to anybody, he could do whatever he wanted. And his life, so far, wasn't so bad, was it? He'd had good times. He'd made people happy and had been made happy by other people and did his share of laughing.

He'd felt it at the wedding, right before the carnage and all, he'd felt just a glimmer of it. But now the full weight of it pressed up against his heart, and it felt pretty damn good.

He laughed. He laughed right out loud.

He was glad to be alive.

It was such a strange, giddy feeling that he had to say it, had to say the words, even though nobody could hear it.

So he said, "I'm glad to be alive, damnit. I'm glad."

Chuckling, he flopped down easily in his beat-up old chair and turned on the lamp next to it.

The electrical current that shot through Henry's body was strong enough to kill him almost instantly. He didn't feel a thing.

Gator Boy

Keegan had tied the rope himself, cinched it tight around the boy's waist, had tousled the straw-blond hair and said *Okay, go get 'em, boy* so he knew there was no one to blame for what happened but himself. The gators were just too fast this time.

And he could say now that he'd had a funny feeling , had a sudden flash of dread as he watched Sammy wade out into the swampy water, watched the gators on the muddy isle perk up. But that could've been hindsight talking.

They'd done it countless times before. The rope, the boy, the gators. Sammy would go out in the water, start splashing around, and it was never long before the gators got interested and came after him. And when they'd get close, Keegan would yank the boy back, right out of the jaws of death as it were, and as the boy scrambled up on the land Keegan would snatch up his bow and let loose with an arrow right into the gator's head.

It worked every goddamn time.

And Keegan himself grew up doing it with his own Pop. His father had taught him how to cinch the rope tight, how to splash around in the water, how to get the gator's attention. He had more than a few scars from his days as the Gator Boy—mostly on his legs and arms but one nice one like a jagged bolt running down his jaw.

Keegan had learned from his own Pop's mistakes. He'd learned the best ways to minimize the danger and keep his Sammy as safe as possible.

Yeah, it worked every time.

Except this time.

The boy had yelled, *They're comin', Pa, they're comin'!* but Keegan had allowed his mind to wander in that one split second, that most crucial second. And then the rope had slipped a little in his callused hands when he yanked on it. Those two things were all the gators needed.

One of them got Sammy by the leg, dragged him under, the whole time the boy screaming *Pa, Pa, help me, Pa!* and then two more dove in on him and the water turned red as they tore him to pieces. And Keegan could only watch in numb horror as his son was devoured.

He stood there on the shore forever and wasn't positive exactly when the cops showed up. But one of them said to him, *You got scars, buddy. I guess you used to do the same thing as your boy there. And you got hurt more than once, by the look of it.*

Numbly, watching the gators now back on the muddy isle, full on the flesh of his son, Keegan said *I really don't mind the scars. They're all I got left,* and the cops put him in the car.

Incident on a Rain-Soaked Corner

Getting shot in real life wasn't anything like what he'd read about in novels. There was no 'lancing pain' or 'sliver of fire' along his torso. There was nothing that specific. What he felt was like someone had shoved him from behind, very hard, pushing him forward and off his feet so unexpectedly that he landed right on his face.

A second later, he heard the crack of a gunshot, echoing up and down the empty city street. At first, he didn't feel anything, just a strange, scared confusion. But then he realized that he couldn't move and his back felt funny and then not so funny at all as the pain exploded and sent little telegrams to his brain and his brain read them, wrote appropriate responses and sent them back. The responses were *Feel it now. Feel the buzz saw along your spine, feel the sensation of having your nerve endings ripped right out and twisted by some ugly metal machine. Feel it? Good.*

He lay there face-down on the sidewalk at the corner, unable to move or speak, and the rain plummeted out of a dark cloud-shrouded night.

His name was Bridges, and he'd been thinking idly about committing murder when he got shot. Only idly, in the sort of off-hand way one thinks about how much easier it would make life if so-and-so was dead, or how that jackass who cut you off in traffic deserved to have a knife stuck in his eye. Nothing serious or heartfelt. He was simply fantasizing.

And the rain started to come down, and he wished he had an umbrella, and he turned the corner onto his street and someone put a bullet in his back.

Face-down on the sidewalk, rain and blood puddling around his head, he finally realized what had happened. He had no memory stored in his databank that correlated to it and that he could draw upon to work out what had happened to him, but he still knew, in a strange, disconnected way. Someone had shot him in the back.

The pain was already fading, which he was aware enough to realize wasn't good. As long as he felt pain, he would be okay. As long as he could feel it, he knew he was still alive. But the pain faded, and he clenched his fingers into claws and tried to grip the sidewalk.

"Help," he said.

He was on the corner, and both streets were silent except for the gentle wash of rain. From where he lay, he could see the intersection, see water gurgling down the grate on the opposite side of the street. The dim glow of the streetlight glimmered a weak hollow yellow, buzzing like a hive of bees in the rain. He tried to lift his head, couldn't.

"Help," he said again, knowing there was no one to hear him.

The pain was almost entirely gone now. His whole body felt numb. He couldn't even feel the rain that pattered down on him. *I'm paralyzed*, he thought. *The bullet tore into my spine and I'm paralyzed and I'll never walk again.*

He started crying, soundlessly. He kept crying until he realized that being paralyzed was probably the least of his concerns.

Wheelchair for the rest of his life? Someone else to cook for him and clean for him and wipe his ass for him? That was nothing. He'd been shot and he was alone on the corner and he was going to die.

"Ah," he said, his voice a hoarse whisper. "Ah, Christ please. Someone help me."

He heard footsteps coming from up the street he'd been about to turn on to. Steady, sure footsteps, and someone whistling cheerfully in the rain.

His heart leapt in his chest, and the pain surged forward like a racehorse. He tried again to lift his head, without success. He gathered what little breath he had and said, "Please. Help."

The footsteps kept coming, closer to where he lay, and he had an awful thought: *what if the person keeps going? What if the person has his head down against the rain, is looking nowhere but straight ahead, and doesn't see me? Or worse, what if the person sees me and just walks on, like one of those horrible city people you always read about who just doesn't want to get involved?*

Or worse yet, what if it's the person who shot me?

But no, it wouldn't be the person who shot him. This person was coming from the other direction. The footsteps kept coming, the whistling louder and louder, and again Bridges said, "Help."

The footsteps stopped very suddenly and the whistling died. Bridges tried to call out again but couldn't. The footsteps resumed, a bit more slowly, coming closer, until a pair of expensive shoes appeared in front of him and stopped. Bridges could see the shoes and the pant legs and the bottom part of a dark raincoat. His fingers scrambled weakly on the sidewalk toward the shoes.

The shoes stepped back a little, and a voice that seemed to come from miles above said, "Well. You don't look so good, friend."

It was a deep, confident voice, like the voice of a really good telephone solicitor. Bridges said, "Ah…" but couldn't manage anything else.

The pant legs went up slightly and the stranger crouched down on his haunches. Bridges could see the open raincoat now, the well-made suit and tie under it. He tried to roll his eyes up to see the face but couldn't manage it.

"What happened to you?" the man said.

"Sh… sh…"

"Shot? You've been shot?"

"Ah."

"Well," the man said. "That's pretty goddamn interesting. It's not often you stroll around the block in the rain and come across someone who's been shot. Wouldn't you say?"

"Help," Bridges wheezed.

"What's that?" the man said.

Bridges squeezed his eyes shut. "Help," he said.

The man chuckled. He actually chuckled. "Help what?"

Bridges was confused. He couldn't think straight. Did this stranger just laugh at him? He was sprawled out on a sidewalk in the rain, a bullet in his back, dying for Christ's sake, and this man laughed at him?

He said, "Please," but the word was barely audible even to his own ears.

The stranger said, "I'm just kidding. You need help, like medical help, right? You're asking me to, I don't know, call an ambulance or something. Right?"

"Please."

"An ambulance, or the cops. Because if you don't get medical attention right away, well, you aren't going to make it. Right? You could die, any second now."

Bridges moved his fingers, trying to reach out and grab hold of the man's pant leg. He couldn't muster the strength.

"And here I am," the man said. "Yakking away while your life bleeds away in the rain. What sort of Good Samaritan am I, huh?" And he laughed again.

He moved a little closer, close enough that he shielded some of the rain from Bridges' head. He said, "Wow. This is really something. Here I am, walking along, and bam, outta nowhere, I stumble across a guy dying from a gunshot in the back. I mean, what are the odds?"

Bridges didn't know the odds, and he didn't care. He was beginning to suspect that this stranger wasn't going to help him.

"So, where'd they get you?" Bridges felt the man's fingers on his shoulder, probing. He felt the fingers travel down his back and come to rest on the place where the bullet had entered.

The man pressed hard on the spot.

"Right here?" he said.

The pain came roaring back, and Bridges cried out weakly and nearly passed out.

The man let go of the spot and gently slapped Bridges on the head. "Don't black out," he said. "You do that, you're not going to wake up again."

Bridges couldn't think through the pain. Every part of him was clenched—his fists against the sidewalk, his eyes squeezed tight, his teeth scraping against each other.

After a long moment, the pain started to recede again and Bridges was sobbing. The stranger crouched there, not moving.

"Wow," he said again. Then, "Hell of a night, huh? They say it's supposed to rain all night."

Bridges said, "Wh…"

"Still, it's good for the trees, right? We haven't had a good rainfall in weeks. It'll really cool things off, I hope."

"Wh… why?"

The stranger said, "Why? Is that what you just said? You really need to speak up, did anyone ever tell you you mumble sometimes?"

"Why?"

"Why, well. That's a good question."

"You... you sh... you sh..."

"Shot you? Me? No, I was just passing by. Funny how things like that will happen sometimes. I don't even know you, buddy. Why would I shoot you?"

"Crazy..."

"Me?" the man said, laughing. "No, I'm not crazy. I'm just a normal guy, like you. Or at least, I assume you're a normal guy. But I could be wrong. Normal guys, as a rule, don't get shot, do they? You must've pissed someone off pretty good, that's all I can figure."

"Help me."

"I am helping you. I'm keeping you company, aren't I?"

"Call... call ambulance..."

He heard the stranger let out a thoughtful breath. "No, I don't think I'll do that, buddy. No ambulance for you."

Bridges said, "Wh... why?"

"Oh, just because. See, I'll tell you a secret, Mr... what's your name, anyway? Oh, never mind, it's not important. I'll tell you a secret."

"Please."

"Hey, you plan on dominating this whole conversation? I let you talk, now it's my turn." He cleared his throat. "See, it's like this. Me, I get up every day at seven. I have a cup of coffee while my wife is still in bed. I take a shower, I shave, I get dressed, and I go to work. Just like everyone else. I work all day for a boss I hate, see. I sell advertising space, if you wondered, but it doesn't really matter. Whatever job you have, you're doing it for someone else, aren't you? In any case, I sell ad space all day long, and some days I do pretty well and other days are a wash-out. I get off at five and I drive home through rush hour traffic and my wife usually has dinner ready, and even though her dinners are barely edible, I eat. While I'm eating, I have to sit there and endure a bunch of mindless small talk about my day and her day. Then I help her with the dishes and I sit down in front of the TV and watch it until ten or so. And then I go to bed."

He didn't say anything for a moment, as if expecting Bridges to comment. A soul-crushing despair had opened up in Bridges' heart and he couldn't say anything even if he'd wanted to.

The man said, "But here's the thing. Here's the thing, buddy. Some nights, I get up in the middle of the night and I put on my coat and I go for a walk. Just around, you know, up and down the street. I walk and I think, and it makes me feel better. Even when it's raining like right now, it always helps. I walk and I think about killing people. You know, just snuffing them right out. I think about stabbing someone or choking them to death or putting them in a wood chipper. Just anybody, you know? Not my wife or my boss or whoever. Just anyone."

Bridges moaned.

"I'm still talking," the man said. "Don't interrupt, okay? I was saying, you know, fantasizing about killing someone just makes me feel better. I've never actually done it before, mind you, and more than likely I never will. But thinking about it, God, it just cheers me right up."

He shifted on his haunches, and the rain shifted too, angling in so that it pelted Bridges directly in the face. The edges of Bridges' vision were dimming.

The man said, "So imagine my delight at finding you out here tonight. I didn't have anything to do with you being shot, but regardless, it's almost like a little slice of my fantasy world just appeared out of nowhere. And the weirdest thing? I had the crappiest day today, you know? I mean, it was worse than usual. Way I figure it, God put you here on this sidewalk, dying with a bullet in your back, so that I would have the strength to go on. God is good, isn't He? He's always there when you need Him."

Bridges could only see the man's shoes and pant legs now. He felt his life slipping away from him.

The man laughed again and said, "Those must seem like pretty hollow words to you right about now, huh? I guess He's not always there for everyone. He's not doing much for you, for instance. Ha."

Bridges felt the man's hand on his back again, slapping him heartily on the hole where the bullet had entered him. It didn't hurt at all this time.

The man said, "The funniest thing about it, to me? You'll never even know who shot you, or why. Right? I mean, was it someone you crossed? Someone you did something to, and you don't even remember? Maybe from years ago. Or maybe it was someone who was going to rob you, but then got scared and ran off. Or maybe it's nothing like that. Maybe it's just some random nut. Just some guy with a gun, wanting to shoot someone. And if that's the case, who can blame him?"

Bridges said, "Bastard." The word came out without hesitation or struggle, which was good, because it would wind up being the last thing he ever said.

The man said, "Bastard? Hey, those are fighting words, mister. You wanna piece of me?" And then he laughed. "I'm kidding again. You can call me whatever you want, that's okay." Then, "Tell you what. I'm on my way home now. I should be there in about ten minutes. When I get in, I'm going to have a drink, maybe read a little bit. And then, just for you, I'll call the cops and tell them I thought I heard a gunshot. That sound okay? I'll tell them I heard shooting, and that they should probably check it out. They'd more than likely find you right away. Okay?"

Bridges didn't say anything. The man's words sounded far away and the imperative to listen to them not near as pressing as before.

"It's the least I can do," the man said. "After all you've done for me. Thanks, buddy."

Bridges' eyes were closed now, but he heard the man stand up, pause for a moment, and then the footsteps were moving away again. He heard them receding down the street, and he heard the soft patter of rain, the gurgling of water rushing down the grate.

And he heard the whistling again, as the man picked up his tune where he'd left off.

Always Too Late

"What if it's already too late?" the woman said. "What if all the things we dread happening have already happened, and it's too late to save us?"

"It's never too late," I said, and she gave me a sort of smirking, half-pitying grin. She shook her head and knocked back the rest of her bourbon and water.

We'd gone out on the veranda, away from the heat and noise of the party inside, and now the night air was cool on our flushed faces and I was very aware of how close she stood to me.

The Belle Isle property stretched out below us, lush and green, and wind rustled through the ornate shrubs and landscaping of our host's private garden.

I said, "What? You think that's naïve of me?"

"Maybe a little," she said. "But maybe some willful optimism is necessary to survive in this world. If we knew the truth, we might just kill ourselves right now and be done with it."

I frowned at her. "That's a pretty bleak assessment."

"It's a pretty bleak world. And believe me, it's going to get bleaker."

"Let's walk," I said, as much to change the subject as anything else. She nodded, and we left the veranda and made our way down to the gardens. She was a tough nut to crack, this one. Very doom and gloom.

Me, I'd always been an optimist, but I'd be lying if I said her pessimism didn't interest me. It seemed to come from someplace deep inside, someplace that actually knew something the rest of us didn't know.

We walked, and I said, "If things are really that bad, there doesn't seem much point in going on, does there?"

She said, "No. Not much point at all," and then, "So why don't I kill myself? That would be your next question, if you weren't so polite. Why don't I end it all, if life is really that awful?"

I didn't say anything, and after a moment she said, "I don't know. I really don't know."

We walked on in silence. The sky above was black and pinpointed with glittering white stars and a warm wind swept through the gardens and pushed her hair into her face. At that moment, she was so beautiful it made me ache. We stopped and I put my hand on the smooth curve of her jaw and kissed her. After a moment, she put her head against my chest and whispered, "You're in danger. You have no way of knowing what's in store for you."

I held her out at arm's length, puzzled.

"I'm sorry," she said. "I'm so very sorry for what's coming. I came here to… to tell you. But it won't do any good, and I'm so sorry."

I started to ask her what she was talking about, but before I could form the words a low, buzzing sound, like a swarm of bees slowly descending, reached my ears. I couldn't tell where it was coming from.

She took a step away from me. "Oh God," she said. "He's here."

"What—"

The buzzing grew louder, and out of nowhere a tiny speck of white light appeared in the air between us. I stepped back from it, and it grew bigger and bigger, a light so raw and white it hurt my eyes. The sound of it was like a roaring now, and I covered my ears. Cold fear gripped me, but I couldn't bring myself to look away.

I couldn't see the girl anymore, just the awful light that got bigger and bigger, until it was the size of a man. And then a figure stepped out of the light. He stepped right out, as simple as crossing a threshold.

A tall, gaunt man with wavy blond hair and a tight-fitting suit. He had a gun in his hand. I stumbled back and fell on the grass. The woman said again, "I'm sorry," but I wasn't sure which of us she was talking to.

The buzzing sound faded, but the horrible white light stayed, like an open door into nowhere. The man stood before it, glaring down at me, his fingers tight around the gun. He spoke, and his voice was like gravel: "I'm disappointed," he said. "I'm so thoroughly disappointed in you, Mona."

"Please," she said. "Don't hurt him."

The buzzing white light hung behind him, and he shook his head. "I'm not going to hurt him. But you, Mona, are coming back with me. You have a lot to answer for."

"No," she said. "Please. I don't want to go back. Please. Can't I stay here?"

"You belong with me."

He grabbed her wrist and started to pull her toward the white light. She fought against him, punching and kicking, but it was no use. I was starting to finally come to my senses. I pushed myself off the ground.

"Leave her alone. I don't know who you are, but she doesn't want to go with you. Leave her."

Struggling with the woman, he snarled at me. "This is not your concern. She shouldn't be here."

I took a careful step toward him, very mindful of the gun in his hand. "Let her go!"

He raised the gun, aimed it at me, and pulled the trigger. The shot boomed across the gardens, and the woman screamed, but I was only vaguely conscious of it. I fell, feeling only a split-second of pain in my spine before total numbness washed over me.

I could hear them fighting, the woman screaming and cursing, as he fought to drag her into the white light that hovered behind them. I heard it all, and could do nothing.

The buzzing, which had faded after the man stepped through the portal of light, started getting louder again, and I could only stare straight up at the night sky, unable to move.

I heard the woman fighting, the sound of a blow, the man grunting in pain and cursing, and then something hard and cold fell on my chest. I was able, barely, to move my right arm. Very slowly, my fingers crawled up my torso, touched the thing on my chest.

The gun.

I took it in my hand, lifted it. I fired blind toward the white light, four, five, six shots. And the light faded and disappeared and I lost the last of my strength and dropped the gun, and the night was again black and silent.

Thirty years went by.

Thirty years, and I sank into some kind of cesspool the likes of which I lack the ability to describe.

Wheelchair-bound, I watched with bitter eyes as the world moved on, away from me, moved on toward some darkness that only I seemed capable of seeing, out there on the horizon.

I had lain there in the grass for over two hours before anyone found me. An ambulance had rushed me to the hospital and surgeons saved my life, but my spine was shattered and when I woke up after surgery the doctor advised me that I'd never walk again.

There were cops, but by the time I was able to see them I'd already made up my mind to not tell them the truth. Who would believe it? I told them I'd been walking the grounds alone, trying to clear my head, when some unknown assailant had appeared out of nowhere, shot me, and ran off.

A puzzling case for them, no doubt. But not near as puzzling as the truth. They investigated, kept the case open for well over a year, but naturally there were no leads and eventually my shooting got marked down as unsolved. One of those 'cold cases' you hear about.

I didn't care. I didn't care about anything. It was too late.

I watched the years stagger by, and every day brought us closer to the destination we'd set our compasses for. And no one seemed to notice. Long, strange years.

In the early 2020's, there was a short-lived nostalgia movement for the 2010's, and a lot of teenage pop stars did their best to sound like their ancient idols.

But with the rise of the Church of Christ Nihilist this movement ended abruptly and the country experienced an alarming spike in parents being murdered by their children to make way for Kingdom Come.

After some hem-hawing, Fox News—"the Only News Allowed by Law"--declared this a step toward a more stable and conservative society.

But after the new right-wing president was assassinated by his own daughter, they re-thought the position and condemned the fervent young Christian Nihilists as 'misguided'.

Technology continued to evolve at a rate faster than humans could keep up with. I'd been in my chair for fifteen years when PC's and laptops suddenly became obsolete and everyone simply had their systems downloaded right into their heads—just a small chip in the left temple, and you could do all your computing and web-surfing from anywhere in the world. The screen would appear in three dimensions, hovering in front of you, invisible to everyone but you, and subtle thought impulses replaced the mouse.

There still wasn't a cure for cancer, though. Or AIDS. Or MS. And no cure for a shattered spine.

I'd been twenty years in the chair when the United States incorporated. By that time, big business made no bones about the fact that they were running the show and had been for decades, so they finally made it official. Without any ceremony, the U.S.I. dissolved the Constitution, took stock of the country's assets, and appointed a CEO and a board of advisors. Share-holders bought in, and within five years every state in the country was contributing to the bank accounts of roughly a hundred very wealthy men. The rest of the country was assigned sliding pay scales, depending on their abilities. The average annual income was anywhere between 20 and 50 thousand.

The unemployed were given a stipend and two years to find steady work. If no job presented itself, they were imprisoned.

The mentally unstable and the hopelessly ill were shipped to rehabilitation centers where they were kept in confinement, feed two meals a day, and allowed out in the sun one hour every two days. This kept roughly a thousand people employed, but was a drain on the share-holder's profits.

If you were incapacitated but happened to have a little money stashed away, like me, the money was confiscated and you were assigned living quarters in what was called Capable Acres—more popularly known as Cripple Ghetto.

The protest movement that sprang up after the incorporation got nipped in the bud early on. Dissidents were 'fired' for insubordination, imprisoned, and sometimes executed.

They dropped nuclear bombs on Iran, Libya, Pakistan and Afghanistan one spring, effectively ending the ongoing hostilities in each of those places, along with the lives of millions of innocent people. This was classified as unfortunate but acceptable losses. Other rogue nations fell quickly into line and all assets were turned over to the U.S.'s shareholders.

A rebellion in Austin, Texas was dealt with in the same manner.

I watched all this from my chair.

I watched in grim isolation, and every single day I thought about the woman, and I thought about the man who had crippled me. I thought and wondered and pondered.

I subscribed to the Head News Feed and scoured it every day.

And then one day, one fine morning thirty years after my spine was shattered, I saw his face.

A billionare. An industrialist. A scientist. And one of U.S.I.' s favorite people.

He'd been instrumental in developing the technology needed to maintain the Corporation's dominance across the globe, but very few people knew he existed. The handful who did speculated—in private, of course—about his work. One of those speculations involved secret projects involving time travel. No one believed it possible.

No one but me.

I had been in contact the last ten years with a small rebel faction based out of the Flint-Detroit Territory. Through a series of carefully encrypted head-mails, I learned that the scientist was in the final stages of a project that could potentially change the course of history.

An area of three square miles, in the middle of the desert that used to be Austin, Texas, was scheduled to be cordoned off for one day. One day, two weeks from now. The project was top-secret, but the name of the billionaire-industrialist-scientist was attached to it.

It took a week for me to secretly arrange travel to Austin, through the rebel faction.

It took the bulk of the second week to work out a way into the desert compound.

They were very helpful, my rebel friends.

That morning, after evading the security forces around the perimeter, they dropped me off in the dusty desert, an old man in an old-fashioned wheelchair, an old man who hadn't smiled in decades and was bent and broken by bitterness and hate.

"Good luck, friend," their leader said to me, before driving away.

They didn't think I'd survive. I didn't think I would either, but it didn't matter. I wheeled through that desert for three hours, sweat pouring from my brow, through the rubble of devastated buildings and playgrounds and freeways, all half-buried in hard black sand.

When I finally came to the site, I was almost disappointed with its simplicity. Nothing but a small clearing, lined with a simple metal gate. Two or three modest machines. A metal fold-out table. That was all. And no scientist. But I wasn't expecting him to be there, not yet anyway.

I unlatched the gate, wheeled through, and positioned my chair facing the empty part of the clearing. I didn't know how long I'd have to wait, but I felt sure it wouldn't be too long.

I waited, and the hazy sun beat down on my head and nothing stirred in the dead desert air.

It wasn't terribly long, fifty minutes by the clock on the arm of my chair. Fifty minutes, and then something shimmered in the air, a very small, white light.

Then the buzzing noise, the buzzing I hadn't heard in thirty years. The white light expanded, the buzzing grew louder, and then he stepped through the portal, dragging the woman behind him.

She was still kicking and fighting and screaming. He yanked her through the portal, cursing, and threw her to the hard ground, and she crumbled there, crying.

I said, "Hello," and he jerked around to face me, startled.

"What..." he said.

"Long time no see. Although for you it's been... what... five seconds?"

The look of bafflement on his face was immensely satisfying. He stood there dumbly, and the warmth of my coming wrath filled me from head to toe and I smiled. I smiled for the first time in thirty goddamn years.

The woman looked up, choking back her tears, and she looked as confused as the scientist. But only for a moment.

Realization dawned on her face, and her eyes grew wide and her mouth curved into something like a grin.

God, she was lovely. For a second I was pulled back across the years, back three decades to when I walked with her through a lush garden in the night, and kissed her lips.

But that was the past, a past that, no matter what sort of machine was invented, would ever exist again.

The scientist said, "How did you… this is a secured area. How did you get here?"

"Not important," I said. "I've come to tell you something. This woman—" and I gestured at her, "—stepped through the ages to reach me, to give me a warning about the future. It didn't have to be me, but it was. And that is your misfortune."

The scientist took a step toward me, hands raised, ready to throttle me, no doubt. From the shimmering white light behind him, six bullets raced through the ages, six bullets on a trajectory through the decades, whining out of the light and into the still hot reality of the desert.

Three of them pounded him in the spine, and one of them blew the back of his skull open. Blood spattered across the black sand and he dropped. But I barely saw it. The last two bullets caught me in the chest.

I slumped back into my chair, the air sucked out of me. I couldn't hear anything, but I was aware of the woman rushing to me. She took my head in her hands and she was crying. Her mouth moved, she was saying something—sorry, maybe?—but it didn't matter. I didn't blame her, not at all. I closed my eyes, felt her lips on mine, felt her hot tears on my face.

I could have loved her, maybe, but it was too late now. It had always been too late.

The Most Natural Thing in the World

The flashlight beam jittered and jerked, and its pale light skipped over black stone, caught glimmers of dust, still drifting down from the cave ceiling like ash. It moved over jagged edges of rock, skimmed across the cave floor, and came to rest on Lex.

Lex whined, cocking her head at the sudden glare. Her front paws shifted, as if she were about to run. But instead she huffed once and settled in the dirt. The flashlight beam wavered on her, and she lowered her head and gazed benignly.

Patrick, slumped against the cave's far wall, held the beam on his dog and said, "Good girl. Good girl, Lexie." Lex made a *hrmph* sound in response to hearing her name, but didn't raise her head.

With trembling fingers, Patrick flicked off the light and the cave again plunged into total darkness. It was uncomfortable, that complete and utter blackness, but he didn't have a choice. The flashlight battery would only last so long.

He placed it carefully on the dirt next to him, leaned his head back against the cold stone, and closed his eyes. He tried not to think about the pain in his right leg. A hunk of stone had come down on it when the walls caved in, and even in the roar of earth shifting around him he'd heard the snap of bone in his thigh and knew it was broken.

The splint he'd tied around it was make-shift, the result of one class, three years ago, on improvised medical emergency treatment. It would keep the break from moving, but it certainly wasn't set properly, and Patrick knew that if he didn't get real medical attention right away, he'd walk with a limp for the rest of his life.

He chuckled bitterly in the darkness. A limp, he thought. Yeah, a limp. That's the least of my goddamn problems right now, isn't it?

The more pressing issue, of course, was the fact that he and Lex were trapped a good fifth of a mile underground, tons of rock and earth above them. And it seemed highly un-goddamn-likely they'd be rescued.

The air was close and heavy, like sticking your head under a thick dark comforter on a sweltering day. Every breath in and out felt labored and hot. Patrick wondered briefly how much air they had left in there, but pushed the thought away. No, no… it would do no good to start worrying about that. It was something he had no control over.

Of course, he had no control over anything presently. The air, the pain in his leg, the dehydration. The hunger.

The hunger most of all. He had no way of keeping track of time, since his watch broke in the cave-in, but he estimated it had been something like five days. All he'd brought along on this little expedition was some water, some dog biscuits for Lex, a bag of crackers and some lunch meat, and they'd eaten all that some time ago.

He'd expected to be back at the motel by early evening.

There was food there, at the motel, in the mini-fridge. Some cold chicken from the previous night's dinner. A box of Cheezie Bits. Some microwave rice, mushroom-flavored.

The thought of all that food, all that fantastic food back at the motel, was almost enough to drive him nuts. He wiped drool off his chin and his stomach twisted and made a loud, unhappy noise.

Oh my God, he thought. So hungry. And poor Lex…

In the darkness, the dog snuffed and shifted, and Patrick groped again for the flashlight. He shined it in Lex's direction, only to see the dog open her eyes and gaze at him with mild curiosity. She sighed and turned her head away from the light.

Lex hadn't come anywhere near him in what seemed like a long time, and that troubled Patrick. Now, in these horrible circumstances, it would be nice to have Lex near him, her narrow head on his lap. It would provide some comfort. But Lex didn't seem to be in need of comfort—at least not from him. It was as if she blamed him for this whole awful ordeal.

Which was a silly notion. Granted, it was his fault, Lex would never have chosen to enter this remote Kentucky cave, but to suppose that Lex knew it was his fault was just ridiculous.

Patrick said, "Hey, Lex. Hey, Lexie old girl." He patted the dirt next to him. "Come on over here with Pop, huh?"

Lex didn't respond.

That worried him. Lex was such a loving, affectionate girl usually. It's hunger, he thought. She's hungry, and doesn't have the energy to get up right now.

The thought of Lex suffering because of his stupidity brought stinging tears to his eyes. He whispered, "I'm sorry, Lexie. I'm sorry, old girl. This is all my fault."

He studied her in the gray glare of the flashlight. She was a great-looking dog, no question. A mutt, but with a strong showing of Golden Lab, and more than a little German Shepard in the thick snout. She was eight years old, and for all eight of those years she'd been Patrick's best friend in the world.

They'd been everywhere together. The road trip to San Francisco. The hiking trip in upstate New York. The fishing trip off the coast of Maine. And now this, this "cave exploring trip" in Kentucky. Old Lexie, always right there by his side, always running when he called, always snuffling up to his hand and licking his palm and looking up at him with calm, sincere affection.

Hunger and fatigue were making him weepy, morose. He wiped tears away from his face with the back of his hand and turned off the flashlight.

In the pitch black, he had nothing but time to think about how stupid this whole situation was. They had told him back in town that this particular network of caves was unsuitable for exploration—they were unstable, shifting constantly. But Patrick, twenty-nine years old, full of overblown and unwarranted confidence in himself, had smiled patiently at the locals and nodded and said nothing. And he'd packed his meager gear and went into the caves anyway.

It would have been pointless to try and explain why these particular tunnels and warrens held appeal for him. It would have been futile to tell them that he wanted to explore these particular caves because they were unsuitable, because other erstwhile explorers had not trod through them. There were other caves, plenty of other caves, that gaped open out of the earth and invited humans to plumb their depths, but Patrick wanted the ones that had to be pried open, forced.

Stretched out now in the dirt, head resting uncomfortably against rock, hemmed in by utter darkness, he felt especially stupid.

His stomach groaned and whined, and a wave of dizziness swept over him. It was a kind of hunger he never knew existed, and he thought with faint amusement now about all those times he'd thought he was hungry, because he'd only had toast for breakfast or had skipped lunch. God, I'm starving, he remembered saying aloud while rummaging through the cupboard for ramen noodles or chicken rice soup or peanut butter, rummaging through the kitchen cupboard that was just jam-packed with any number of good things to eat.

If I could go back in time, he thought. If I could go back in time, I'd slap the shit out of that other version of me and I'd eat every goddamn thing in the cupboard.

He was aware that starvation would be his likely cause of death. It was impossible not to think about. Whenever his mind drifted off to something else, his stomach would send up a telegram to his brain, a little friendly reminder.

In a bout of helpless frustration, he pounded his fists against the dirt, like a kid throwing a temper tantrum.

A sharp pain stung his left forearm, and he sucked in breath, wincing. His right hand went immediately to the spot where the pain had bloomed, and he felt wetness there.

Damnit, he thought. Ah, Christ, what the hell…

He heard Lex shifting in the dark a few feet away from him. With his right hand, he groped for the flashlight, found it, snapped it on. He focused the beam on his left arm and saw that his sleeve was ripped open and blood dripped from a slight gash. The face of the wall next to him was jagged and sharp with protruding rock, and he'd managed to slice his arm open on it during his little fit.

Idiot, he thought. Nice going, asshole.

He started to reach for his knapsack, resting on the other side of his head, to find something to staunch the flow of blood, when he heard a low, dangerous growl from the darkness.

He shot the flashlight beam in Lex's direction, and his heart nearly stopped.

Lex was on her feet, crouched ever so slightly, and her gaze was fixed directly on Patrick. Her tail was stiff behind her. Her lips pulled back, exposing her sharp yellow teeth, and she growled menacingly.

Patrick's blood went cold. He kept the light trained on Lex, and the dog only stared at him, the growl a low rumble deep in her throat.

"Lexie?" he whispered. "Lexie."

Lex took a cautious step toward him, and for the first time in the eight years they'd been together Patrick saw his dog as a predator. He saw her as a hunter and a killer. He saw her in the natural state of all canines, the prehistoric state, twenty or thirty thousand years ago, before humans learned to domesticate them and train them. He saw her as what she might have been.

"Lexie," he said again. "Girl. Hey, girl. It's me."

His bladder felt tight, even though he hadn't had a drop of water in a long time. It had never occurred to him before, the idea that Lex—his dog, his friend—was quite capable of killing him.

Lex took another step toward him, and Patrick saw thick ropes of saliva drooping from her jaws.

She's as hungry as I am. Maybe hungrier. She's not herself anymore. And then—the blood! It's the blood, dripping from my arm! She can smell it, that's why she's doing this, that's why, it's not her fault, it's the smell of blood!

He said, "Okay, Lexie. It's okay, girl." Slowly, keeping the light trained on her, he reached into his knapsack and rooted around until his fingers closed on a soiled bandanna. He pulled it out and, setting the flashlight carefully on his lap with the beam still focused on Lex, he wrapped it quickly around his wounded forearm.

The cut had been just deep enough to draw out a sudden gush of blood, but already the bleeding had started to slow down. Shivering, Patrick kept his eyes on Lex as he tightened the makeshift tourniquet with his teeth and took up the flashlight again.

"See?" he said. "All better, girl. No more… no more blood."

Lex continued to growl, but her body relaxed somewhat. The stiff tail went down, the bared teeth withdrew behind her lips. Bit by bit, the tensed muscles of her body eased, until her intense and hungry stare finally broke off and she glanced around the dark cave.

"See?" Patrick said again. "It's okay now, right?"

Lex's growl diminished into a weary sigh. She snorted and dropped her head. She turned away from him and dropped to the rock-strewn ground, sighing again.

Patrick released the long breath he hadn't realized he was holding, and the beam of light on Lex started trembling. Oh my God, he thought. Oh my dear Christ, Lex was going to… she was ready to…

But his mind veered away from it. It was too horrible to even contemplate.

He felt fresh tears in his eyes and was uncertain which emotion they'd come from—sorrow or fear. He found he was reluctant to turn off the flashlight, to remove its stark glare from Lex's still form.

Lex, he thought. Oh Lex, my poor girl. What have I done to you?

Eventually, when it looked like Lex had fallen asleep, he forced himself to turn off the light. He lay there in the pitch black, holding the flashlight in a fierce grip, too terrified to close his eyes. He had never felt so completely defenseless in his life, propped up like a department store mannequin against the cold rock, his leg useless, his body too weak from hunger to even move.

If Lex should lose it, he thought… if Lex loses it, what can I do? Nothing. She could kill me easily. I'd be Alpo with legs.

But she wouldn't. She'd come to her senses before hurting me, yes. She's hungry, but Christ… we're best friends. She would get a hold of herself.

He almost laughed at that notion, knowing it was bullshit. Lex was a dog, an animal, and instinct had a way of kicking in with animals. Family ties, love, devotion… all those things existed for a dog, certainly, but all it would take is one moment, one instant of madness and hunger, for all those learned traits to disappear.

If she got hungry enough, Lex would attack him. Lex would eat him.

And Patrick started thinking of his best friend in a different light now. He started thinking of her as a potential enemy.

Lex had been a gift, seven years ago, from Ellie. Ellie, whom Patrick had been ready to marry at the time. A gift for their… what was it? Third anniversary together, yeah. Three years of bliss and great sex and stupid arguments, and Ellie had gone to the animal shelter and found the adorable little puppy and cut holes in the top of a box and presented it to Patrick.

"You keep saying how much you love dogs," she'd said. And he did. He opened the box and little Lexie had come popping out of it like a spring toy, tail wagging in hysterical joy, instantly jumping into Patrick's lap and licking his face and woofing happily. They were best friends, right from the word go.

The irony of it, when things finally ended between him and Ellie five months later, was Ellie telling him he was incapable of loving another human being the way he loved his dog. "If you gave half as much affection to me as you do to Lex..." she'd said, and three and a half years went down the drain.

But Patrick didn't miss her much. He had Lex, and Lex was all he needed.

Still... he hadn't had a serious relationship with a woman since then. And there were obviously certain benefits to someone like Ellie, certain benefits that a canine companion couldn't compensate for.

He spoke into the darkness, his voice hoarse, "Say, Lexie. You remember Ellie, don't you? Old Ellie. Good ole Ellie."

Lex didn't respond.

Patrick said, "She had great tits." He laughed weakly. "And great taste in dogs. She... she's the one who picked you out, you know. Did you know that?"

Silence from the darkness.

"You... you probably don't remember her," Patrick said. "It was a long time ago."

His stomach rumbled and whined, and another wave of dizzy nausea passed through him.

So hungry. So goddamn hungry.

He thought, of course Lex doesn't remember her. Lex is a dog. Lex is a stupid animal with no thought of the past or the future or anything except the moment she lives in. Lex doesn't think of anything except food and running and playing and more food. Lex is a creature who, whenever you leave the room for half a minute and come back, she reacts as if she believed she'd never see you again and goes crazy with joy that you're back.

Lex is a beast. A dumb brute.

My best friend, he thought, is a dumb brute, with no conscience or sense of right and wrong, other than what I've instilled in her through punishment and reward.

Her love for me is based on what I feed her.

Christ…

A sort of madness had seized Patrick's brain as he lay there in the darkness, a sort of ugly epiphany. Lex was not his friend. The love they shared was a lie. He fed her and she provided companionship, companionship he needed in lieu of another human being in his life. It was all an ugly, pathetic lie.

Somewhere deep inside him, the realization sparked a glimmer of sorrow, but it was overridden by rage. The dog fooled me, he thought. The dog tricked me into loving her. The bitch.

He squeezed his eyes shut and gritted his teeth and imagined her, only feet away from him, laying there in the dark watching him, waiting for the opportunity to spring upon him. Waiting for the chance to seize him by the throat and kill him.

He smiled an ugly, bitter smile.

Oh, you think so, do you? You think you're gonna kill me, you stupid dog? Better think again.

Shifting his weight, he reached inside his jeans pocket with his free hand and felt the Swiss Army knife there. He pulled it out and flicked open the cutting blade. It wasn't much of a weapon, less than two inches long, but it would do the trick. Bury it right in Lex's throat, right under the snout, and it would kill her as thoroughly as any machete.

Who's gonna eat who, he thought. Who's the smart one here, Lex? Who's the one who can actually think?

Raw dog meat. Well, it didn't sound particularly appetizing, even as hungry as he was. But he could probably choke it down, in a pinch. Sure. Use the knife to skin her, take your time, cut out a few choice pieces, chow down.

"Ha," he said, and it echoed chillingly in the dark cave.

He flicked on the flashlight again and the beam shone in Lex's face. She was staring at him, and her eyes were big and blank, like doll's eyes, or like black buttons on an overcoat. Her left ear twitched.

The beam started shaking again.

Lex looked so innocent. She looked innocent and hungry and scared. Patrick began crying.

"I'm sorry," he moaned. "Oh, Lexie, girl, I'm so sorry."

He dropped the knife on his lap, let the flashlight beam drop and lapsed into an almost hysterical fit of remorse. Sobs racked his body painfully and he wailed and moaned and cursed himself. Lex watched him with empty eyes.

After a very long time, he began to pull himself together. The sobs degenerated into weak snuffing and sniffling, and finally he took a deep breath and again shone the flashlight on Lex.

Lex cocked her head, stood up slowly. She stretched expansively, snorted, sighed, and gazed at him.

Patrick said, "Lexie. Come over here, huh?"

Lex ambled around the small dark space, and for a moment Patrick feared that she might have gone loopy. Her wandering seemed strangely aimless. But finally she came near him and settled down next to his broken leg. With a weary huff, she rested her head on the make-shift splint.

Even that slight weight hurt his leg, but he winced and didn't move. The pain was worth it, just to have her next to him again.

He rubbed her head and scratched her behind the ear, just the way she loved it. She closed her eyes and pushed her head against his fingers, and Patrick realized how this all had to end.

We are both going to die, he thought. Barring some miracle rescue, we are both going to die of starvation and dehydration. It's just a question of which one of us will die first.

And the one who dies first, without question, will become a meal for the other. It was just the most natural thing in the world, and there was nothing for it.

Patrick wiped snot away from his nose with the back of his hand. He placed the flashlight on the side of him opposite Lex, unmindful now of the battery. He picked up his Swiss Army knife and gazed at it for a long moment, his other hand still scratching behind Lex's ear.

He plunged the blade into his own throat and felt Lex jump against him and then blood was choking him and he couldn't breathe. The knife fell from his fingers and Lex started barking but the sound of it faded away quickly, much quicker than he would have expected, and he slumped over onto the hard ground and the flashlight rolled away.

Lex barked and barked and barked.

Many, many days later, rescuers managed to dig their way in. They were met by a raving, blood-thirsty brute that tried to attack them the second they punched a hole through the rocks. When they saw what else was in the cave, one man vomited and they immediately sent back up for a rifle. They gave it to the bravest of the rescuers, and he unceremoniously put a bullet through the beast's brain.

Heart

I'd been dead for three years before I realized it. That whole time, walking around, going to work (sometimes), making small talk when I had to, forced smile etched on my face. Not a clue I was a fucking corpse. Feeling something missing inside me, sure, but not really… you know. Not really getting it.

It took the aftermath of the last big crack-up with Molly for it all to sink it. I was dead, and had been for three long, miserable years.

Five days after the fight, after I'd walked out of the house, swearing I'd never come back, I was still drinking. But I couldn't get drunk no matter how much I tried. The cold hard center of sobriety held sway over my dead brain, and resisted every assault against it.

The bartender had been eyeing me for the last five minutes as I put back shot after shot of whiskey. He set a third beer in front of me, said, "This is the third day in a row I've seen you here, brother."

"Yeah. So?"

"And you're wearing the same damn clothes."

I looked around at the other patrons. Not a fashionista in sight. I said, "There a dress code here?"

"No, brother. It's not the sight of your clothes that's bugging me. It's the smell. You dig?"

"So I stink. So what?"

"So no one else wants to sit at my bar, brother. You're stinking my customers out."

If someone had said that to me three years ago, I'd have been mortified. But now I didn't care, not at all. So I smelled bad. So fucking what? Do you expect a corpse to smell like roses?

"And so," the bartender said. "I'm gonna ask you to finish that beer, and be on your way. No trouble, right?"

I shrugged. "Okay," I said. I suppose I could've argued the point, but I didn't care about that, either.

I just didn't care about anything anymore.

I finished my beer, got up, threw a fiver on the bar and walked out on steady legs.

Drinking wasn't really my thing. Honestly, I'd never been big on it, aside from a couple years of partying in my early '20's. Booze always gave me a headache, and I never liked that fuzzy feeling that comes with drunkenness. But things were different now. I was dead inside and booze had no effect on me anymore.

So why bother drinking? Good question. Outside the bar, I decided to stop it.

Which meant I had to think of something else to do with my time. There was no home for me with Molly anymore. There was no job, either—I'd walked in at nine o'clock on the morning after the blow-out, went into Mr. Durkman's office, and pissed on his desk. Yeah, literally whipped out my dick and pissed all over his teakwood. Said, "I hope you'll kindly accept my resignation," then walked out before he could get his jaw off the floor.

I'd had fantasies about doing that. The fantasies made me smile. But actually doing it… didn't feel like anything.

I walked up the street away from the bar, toward the park where I'd slept the night before. It was a decent suburban neighborhood, and I remembered wondering how long it would be before the cops came and rousted me, but they never did.

My stomach grumbled as I walked, and it dawned on me that I hadn't eaten in a while. How long? Wasn't sure. It must've been yesterday sometime. A hot dog, maybe, from the vendor in front of the bank? That sounded right. I didn't want to eat, didn't derive any pleasure from the thought of it, but I knew enough to realize I had to get a little food in me or my stomach wouldn't shut up and leave me alone.

Fingers fumbling in my filthy pants pocket found a ten dollar bill and a couple ones. I looked at them, frowning. That was it. That was all my money, right there. Didn't I have almost two hundred bucks a couple days ago?

I had a bank account. Or rather, me and Molly did. A joint account, even though, after my first marriage ended I swore I'd never do anything like that again. My first wife, Alana, absolutely took me to the cleaners after the divorce, claiming the entire twenty thousand we'd saved as well as spousal and child support.

Child support for my boy, Jim. Eleven years old now. I hadn't seen him in eight. The court ruled in Alana's favor on that one. It didn't matter that it was an accident, that I was only trying to spank him and I didn't mean to hurt him in his... in his private parts. It was a fucking accident. But Alana made it sound like I did it on purpose and the judge was conflicted enough that he didn't convict me. But he did forbid me from having contact.

I used to cry about that, sometimes. But that was a long time ago. These days when I thought of Jim, I didn't feel anything at all.

So the joint account with Molly. I could've made my way over to the credit union—it was only a few blocks south—to withdrawal some cash. But I didn't want to. I didn't want any of that money. It had a taint on it that I couldn't explain. Molly could have it all, for all I cared.

Lying, cheating Molly.

We met two years after my divorce, during that weird transitional period when I was beginning to pick up all my body parts and start stitching them back together into something that vaguely resembled what I used to be. I'd dated four or five women in that period—well, dated isn't the right word. Fucked, that's what I'm trying to say. I couldn't get interested in anyone enough to take it beyond that. Until Molly.

It was my fourth job in that two year stretch, this one at a mall book store (a dying breed, that). She came in the store, with her black hair streaked with purple, her geeky glasses and big boots. Ten years younger than me. Looking for Lolita, by Nabokov. And something happened in my guts, some bizarre feeling that had been missing for so long I didn't even recognize it.

I told her something about how I loved Lolita and next thing you know we're talking and talking and when I got off work we met for a drink and went back to the motel room I'd been staying at. The next night we wound up at her apartment.

And six months later, we were married.

Six months after that, I started seeing the signs, the little subtle hints, that she was cheating on me. And would you believe I tried to ignore it? I really did. I just didn't want to know, I didn't want to go through another tragic ending, because I wasn't sure if I could survive it.

I didn't survive it. I died when it finally happened.

But no, that's not really true. I was dead already, like I said before. That stitched-up Frankenstein monster was never really alive, never really a creature that could feel anything human, not like before.

So I couldn't blame Molly. She didn't kill me. That little spark of life I felt when we first met was an illusion. It was some biological process, like gas escaping from a bloated corpse. That's all.

At the hot dog stand I ordered one dog, mustard, onions. The guy served it up, looking at me sideways, and as he handed it over I was horrified to realize the look on his face was pity.

He said, "Hey, buddy. No charge for that, okay? You look pretty hungry."

"What do you mean?" I said. "What do you mean, no charge?"

"I mean, it's on me. On the house."

"What? You think I can't afford it? You think I can't afford one little stupid fucking hot dog?"

"No, I mean… I'm just saying."

I threw the ten dollar bill at his stupid, smug face. He flinched. I said, "Fuck you. You hear me? Fuck you and your stupid fucking charity!" And then I threw the hot dog at him.

Mustard spattered all over his face, onions down his shirt. He sputtered, and I reached over the stand and grabbed him by the labels and head-butted him. It made a solid chunk sound, solid enough to send him reeling backward when I let go of him. He stumbled two, three steps and fell on his ass.

In a heartbeat I was around the stand and pummeling him.

I was vaguely aware of people gathering around us, voices raised in alarm. I pounded my fist into the vendor's face over and over again, and my head was clear and my thoughts were like crystal. This was no mad rage. This was studied and exact, an almost clinical doling out of vengeance. I even knew he didn't deserve it, but so what? I didn't deserve what happened to me, did I? No one deserves anything but to be left alone in peace, to seek out some simple, vapid happiness. But no one ever gets to do that, do they? No one ever gets to do that.

At the sound of approaching police sirens, I finally let the vendor go and his limp body slumped to the pavement. Blood bubbled from between his lips and he moaned softly but didn't open his eyes. I looked around. There were about ten or twelve people standing there, watching. None of them had done anything to help the vendor. They only watched. Two of them were filming the whole thing on their smart phones. Maybe I'd wind up on Youtube.

I walked away.

It didn't take long for me to realize I needed to find someplace other than the park to crash that night. No doubt the cops would be looking for me, at long last. I'd gone suddenly from being a harmless, broken man sleeping rough to being a violent nutcase—they'd have to do something about me now.

So I walked and walked, and I thought. And I marveled a little at this cold thing my heart had become. When you're dead, you can still remember what life felt like, you know? You can still remember how it feels to know love, or rage, or fear. That's the great tragedy of being dead. Remembering. But remembering the way you'd remember a movie you saw once. Interested in it, yes, but not… invested. It doesn't touch you in any profound way.

I was dead and I didn't care.

But I did need money. Throwing my last ten dollar bill at the vendor had been a stupid move. I could get by with stealing food, if I had to, but the whole episode had left me drained and tired. As night came rolling in, the rumbling in my stomach grew more insistent, and I knew I'd have to eat soon or pass out right there on the street.

I walked through the night, trusting to providence to provide me with an answer. Providence didn't let me down.

It was almost three in the morning, and I'd been walking for what seemed like years. My feet were swollen in my shoes, my stomach tied in knots of hunger, my throat dry and my head pounding. My eyes had been downcast, mostly, watching the dirty and broken sidewalk get dirtier and more broken. And when I finally looked up, I was a little surprised to find that I'd walked all the way to the East side, the absolute worst part of town. It was a dark, deserted street in an industrial area, the only light coming from a flickering streetlamp at the farthest corner, and not a soul around.

Not a soul, except for the thin, nervous young man leaning against the sheet metal wall of a factory.

"Hey," he said, with a slight nod. He wore tight jeans and one of those cut-off tee-shirts showing off a scrawny midriff. Mascara outlined his big blinking eyes.

"Hey," I said back to him. I smiled.

He sniffed, ran the back of his hand under his nose. "Lookin' for a date?" he said.

I nodded. "Yeah. Yeah, man, I sure am."

"Okay," he said. "Come over here." He managed a sickly grin and started into an alley that ran behind him.

Hands in pockets, I followed.

A few feet in, he faced me, moved in close, put his hand on my crotch. "You want me to suck it?" he said. "Or you got somethin' more serious in mind?"

"Something more serious," I said.

I grabbed him by the throat with my dead man's hands.

He started to scream right away, but I slammed him against the wall and his breath wheezed out, stinking of cigarettes and spearmint gum. He started to slump, but I held him up, smashed my fist into his nose. It sounded like a vase being broken under a cushion, and blood washed hot over my fingers. I hit him again, the second time getting less crunch and less blood. His eyes rolled back.

I jabbed him in the gut and he didn't even have enough breath left to grunt. I let him fall that time, kicked him in the head once on the way down. When he was sprawled on the concrete I kicked him again, and then again, in the face and neck.

While he lay there, unmoving except for the shallow rise and fall of his frail chest, I stepped back, breathing hard. I glanced around the alley. A few feet away, I spied a broken beer bottle.

I staggered over to it, picked it up. I staggered back.

He looked up at me with blank eyes, not even enough strength to beg for mercy.

I started in with the broken bottle.

Three minutes later I was done and he was nothing but a scattered mess of blood and ruined flesh. I was on my knees over him, and my throat was raw and I realized I'd been screeching and wailing the whole time, like some mad banshee. I was covered with his blood. Pieces of him were on my shirt and in my hair and he was not the young man he'd been, not anymore. He wasn't anything.

I'd taken it all away from him. Just like Molly had taken it all away from me.

"There," I screamed at him. "There. How do you like it? How do you like it?"

And I realized there were tears in my eyes. No, not just tears. I was bawling. I was sobbing like a baby.

"Goddamnit!" I screamed at the corpse. "Goddamnit!"

Because I wasn't dead. I wasn't dead, after all.

I was alive, and that was worse.

The Bad Little Pet

Peter Lampner lived in his new two-bedroom house for almost three days before he first saw the thing he came to know as The Shape. It was big and black and indistinct, and seemed to grow from the corner of his vision like a creeping cataract.

He was in bed, half-asleep, when The Shape loomed out of the darkness on the far side of the bedroom and glided silently toward him. He peered at it through half-closed eyes with the sort of numbness that accompanies a half-awake state. He didn't feel fear, exactly, but an uneasy, muddled confusion.

The Shape was an enormous mass of dark disconnecting itself from the shadows. It seemed to hover over Peter's bed, and Peter began coming truly awake then, chills playing along his arms and something like terror gripping him. He thought, oh crap a ghost a demon holy crap who would have thought am I going to die?

Part of The Shape—only part of it—came toward his face and he flinched away, pressing the back of his head into his pillow. It's going to strangle me, he thought. It's going to wrap that inky blackness around my throat and throttle the life right out of me. He squeezed his eyes shut, felt The Shape near him, felt the part of it that came toward his face…

Felt it brush against his hair.

Felt it… brush against my hair?

Gently.

Lovingly, even.

The Shape stroked his head with a sweet, kind caress, its black formlessness cool on his brow. Peter opened his eyes and gazed up at The Shape. It was still only a gently swirling mass of black, its edges indefinable and obscure, that seemed to take up all but the very edges of Peter's vision.

He sensed something coming off it in undulating waves. Something… content? Kind?

As The Shape lovingly stroked his hair, Peter thought—with an insight that wasn't much like him, really—that this being could crush him if it so chose. It could utterly destroy him in a fit of pique or anger. But instead it loved him, or at the very least felt something like calm affection.

And so Peter felt himself drifting back into sleep, with The Shape stroking his brow, and he felt the contentedness and kindness of The Shape with each gentle stroke, and right before falling entirely back into slumber Peter felt something else, too.

He felt the soft velvet chains of being completely and irretrievably owned.

He worked in the accounts receivable department of a big office downtown. The next day, in the break room, he mentioned the dream (because by that time he'd become certain it was a dream) about The Shape.

Rich, the guy who occupied the cubicle next to his, said, "Shape? Hey, man, was it Natalie Portman? 'Cuz I had a dream about her the other night, did I tell you?"

"Yeah, Rich, you mentioned that."

"Right. Was it Natalie Portman in your dream?"

"No. It was just a shape, you know, all big and black—"

"Big and black?" Chuck said. Chuck actually worked in customer service, but the three of them generally took lunch together. "Big and black? Say, Peter, you trying to tell us something?"

Chuck and Rich laughed heartily, and Peter smiled with the patience he'd learned after so many years with the two of them.

"Yeah," Rich said. "Did the shape look like Samuel L. Jackson, maybe? Or Denzel Washington? You got a thing for the brothers now, Peter?"

Laughter all around, and Peter forced himself to chuckle good-naturedly. Why, he thought, did I bother to bring it up to these two morons? His head hurt a bit and he wished he'd sat somewhere else for lunch.

"Yeah," he said. "I got a thing for the brothers now. Once you go black, right?" and Chuck and Rich laughed and laughed and laughed and slapped Peter on the back.

It was his first house after renting for most of his life, and at thirty-three his parents and friends thought it was long overdue. "Grown-ups own, son," Dad had said. "This renting business, it's for the birds. Think of all the money you've funneled right into some landlord's back pocket ever since you left home. All that money could have gone into a place of your own, a place you could really call home."

Peter didn't argue, although he saw very little difference between funneling money into a landlord's back pocket and funneling money into a bank's loan department for the next thirty years of his life. Who really cared? But for the sake of peaceful family relations, he'd taken the small suburban house just four minutes from the freeway when the real estate agent offered him a deal.

They were standing in the small kitchen, after taking five minutes to tour the house and admire the new windows and faucets, discussing the water pressure and the hardwood floors and the Michigan basement. The agent—a rather bony woman, middle-aged, with the smell of stale cigarette smoke clinging to her company blazer—had said, "The lady who lived here before was a real character. Never married, the whole forty-odd years she lived here. Always had cats, though."

"Oh," Peter had said. "Like a crazy cat-lady kind of thing, right?"

"Well, not exactly. Not tons of cats running around or anything like that. As far as I know, she only ever had one at a time. Her name was Mrs. Semple. Passed away about a year ago." The agent looked at Peter sharply, as if she'd just caught herself before stumbling off a cliff, and said, "Not in the home, though, heavens no. She passed away in a nursing home downtown." Then, almost as an afterthought, "God bless her, huh?"

"Yeah, God bless her."

The agent had said, "So what do you think?" and Peter said he thought it was just fine and the agent smiled broadly and shook his hand.

Two weeks and thousands of pages of signed documents later, Peter moved into his new home.

Like everything else that had ever happened to him, Peter felt barely in control of the whole process. He felt—when he actually took the time to think about it—that he actually had very little influence in the direction his life took; things just sort of happened and if you didn't want to go completely insane you just sat back and let it go. He envied those guys who seemed so on top of things, so… in charge. How do they do it, he would ask himself some nights, when the feeling of being a tiny boat in a huge ocean would almost overwhelm him. How do they do it? How do they wrest control of their own worlds from the iron grip of fate and circumstance?

If I knew that, Jenna would never have left me.

So he would shrug mentally and roll over and drift into sleep, thinking, that's a question for better men than me.

When he made it home from work, with twilight just settling in and slinking gray light touching the walls, he found his dinner waiting on the table.

He set his briefcase on the kitchen floor next to him and stared dully.

Dinner?

It looked like… chicken. Half a chicken, roasted, with a steaming baked potato and lightly steamed broccoli.

His favorite.

He'd had a headache all day, and now… Uneasily, Peter glanced around the kitchen, saw no signs of anyone having been there—no dirty dishes, no clutter, no nothing—except the dinner, still hot, judging from the steam drifting off the potato.

He said, softly, "Hello?" Then, with more force, "Anybody here?"

No answer.

It's a prank, Peter thought. One of the guys is lurking somewhere in the house, maybe in the bedroom, struggling to keep from laughing out loud. A weird prank, to be sure, and more than a little irritating, but what else could it be?

Peter backed away from the meal on the table and went into the bedroom. Empty. He tried the bathroom, the study, back into the living room to look behind the couch. He even opened the door to the basement and peered down into the darkness before deciding no one would be so dedicated to a practical joke they would hide in the pitch blackness down there until Peter arrived home.

Peter was alone in the house, alone with the meal that had seemingly appeared out of nowhere… the meal that smelled really, really good.

He went back into the kitchen and stood in the doorway staring at the chicken and potato and broccoli.

"Huh," he said.

When was the last time I came home and found dinner waiting for me? When was the last time someone cared that much? Even Jenna had never done anything like that for him before.

And damn, it smells great.

He was salivating and before he knew it he had sat at the table and began eating.

And it was delicious.

Half-asleep that night, The Shape again came to him, stroking his hair and purring soft words of affection. Peter smiled, stretched luxuriously in his bed, and fell into sleep with the soft blackness caressing his forehead.

He awoke the next morning to find breakfast waiting for him.

"You disappoint me," Jenna had said. "But I suppose I should be used to it by now."

They were sitting in his old living room, only days before he moved into the new house, and boxes of his belongings surrounded the ratty sofa he'd owned for too many years. He'd done all the packing himself. Jenna was conveniently out of town during most of that time, and Chuck and Rich couldn't be reached.

She'd said the words without rancor, almost with a resigned sadness. It would have hurt if Peter hadn't been immune to it by now.

"If you'd only said yes," Jenna continued, not looking at him. She sipped her glass of wine and pulled away when he tried to scooch closer to her. "Your boss already has doubts about you, why would you give him more ammo?"

"I'm not interested in taking over any new accounting contracts. How many times do I have to say it?"

"It's not a matter of being interested, Peter, it's a matter of showing you have initiative. How do ever expect to get ahead with the company if you don't tackle new challenges?"

"What makes you think I'm interested in getting ahead? I like my position just fine."

She scowled at him. He was used to the scowl. She never really looked at him anymore, not without the scowl. "Well, that's just great, Peter. Don't worry about the future, God no. They're outsourcing low level jobs like yours all the time, don't you know that?"

"They aren't going to out—"

"The only ones who make it, Peter, are the ones who step up to bat. The ones who take the bull by the horns and wrestle some personal control over their lives. When we first met—"

"When we first met," Peter interrupted, "I told you I wasn't a career-minded kind of guy. I don't live to work, you know, I—"

"If you say I work to live, I swear to God I'll scream."

And so they'd sat in silence for a few minutes.

When Jenna finally stood up, he watched her with a sort of dead expression on his face and she'd said, "I don't know, Peter. I… I need to think. I need to think about us, about where we're going as a couple. You can't just coast through life, just letting things happen. You're a man. I wish you'd start acting like one."

She left, and Peter only saw her twice after that. Once, right before he moved, when she came by to tell him she'd thought it over and believed they needed some time apart, and then again, when they met for coffee and she said she'd wanted to see if he'd made any changes in his life or had thought things over.

"You're destined for mediocrity, Peter," she said, long after he felt she had the right to say such a thing to him. "Life is just going to… happen to you."

Again, dinner awaited him when he arrived home from work. Steak this time, with French-fried potatoes and a spinach salad. A can of beer sat next to a frosted glass by the plate.

Peter smiled through the pain in his temples, setting down his briefcase, stomach rumbling. He didn't remember buying a steak last time he went grocery shopping, but who cared? One never argues with steak.

He loosened his tie and sat down to eat. The steak was perfect, cooked medium-well, just as he liked it. He made appreciative noises, gobbling it down, not bothering to pour the beer into the glass, just drinking right out of the can.

About halfway through the meal, The Shape appeared. Hazy and indistinct as usual, it seemed to take up the whole corner of the kitchen, by the stove. Peter placed his knife and fork down gently on the plate, slowly chewed the piece of meat in his mouth. The Shape hovered patiently.

Finally, Peter said, "Thank you."

The Shape buzzed deeply, vibrating the floor. Peter felt it through his shoes.

He said again, "Thank you. For dinner."

The Shape gave off pleasant echoes of emotion, pleased.

"You… you're very good to me," Peter said. "I don't know why. And I don't know who you are, but… you're very kind. Thank you."

The Shape made a sound that made Peter think of sonic echoes underwater, the sort whales make. It was deep but gentle and anything but threatening. A word seemed to rise up out of the depths, a word that sounded like Petey.

Peter said, "It's Peter, actually. I… um. I don't really care to be called Petey."

And again, from the depths of The Shape, Petey.

It moved across the kitchen toward him, an enormous approaching black hole. It stroked his neck and his shoulder, scratched him gently behind the ear. It rubbed his temples.

"Ha," Peter said. "That feels nice. Thank you."

He picked up his fork again and started back in on the steak. While he ate, The Shape loomed nearby, like a protective parent.

He'd just popped some aspirin and was getting ready for bed when his mother and father called to tell him some wonderful news.

"Your little brother just got a full scholarship!" Dad's voice fuzzed out at the end, his excitement causing him to speak much louder than necessary. "Isn't that fantastic?"

His mother, apparently on the upstairs extension, said, "We're so proud, and I know you are too, Peter. Isn't that just wonderful?"

"Hey, that's great," Peter said. And it was great news, certainly...

"We always knew that boy was gonna be a great one," Dad said. "He studied so hard, and with so much dedication. You know what it is, Peter? The complete refusal to be anything less than the best. That's what marked Jeff, right from the start. Wasn't I just saying that, Maggie? Wasn't I just saying that about our Jeff?"

"You sure were," Mom said.

Peter's little brother Jeff had been an exceptional student from his first day in pre-school. His high school years were cluttered with trophies and awards and certificates, all testifying to his absolute superiority over everyone else—including Peter. And now, a full scholarship to the prestigious university he'd always dreamed of attending, followed no doubt, by a brilliant career in engineering.

Jeff would invent things. He would become, perhaps, one of the most famous and successful engineers in the world, forever changing the way the world lived and worked.

And Peter couldn't help himself. He said, "That's really terrific, you guys, man, I'm so proud of my baby bro, you wouldn't believe it. But…" He cleared his throat. "You know, they're saying, with this economy, things are gonna get worse, you know? I mean, my generation is the first in the history of this country—except maybe for the Great Depression—that's actually poorer than their parents. You know that, right? Little Jeff is brilliant, yeah, but what good will that do him if—"

"Damn right he's brilliant," Dad said. "And that brilliance will see him through, none of these 'bad economy' excuses for him. He's gonna be something, you mark my words. The boy's got ambition."

Mom seemed to pick up on Peter's bout of insecurity. She said, "Yes, we're proud of Jeff. We're proud of both our boys, aren't we, Art?"

"Hmph," Dad said. "Sure we are."

"Both our boys are very… special, yes they are. You've done quite well for yourself, Peter, I don't care what anyone says. And it doesn't matter, your father and I love you no matter what. Don't we, Art?"

"Yeah, of course."

Peter swallowed hard and said, "Sure, sure. Well, tell Jeff I said way to go, okay? I've really gotta get going. Long day tomorrow, should get to bed."

"We'll tell him, Peter," Mom said. "We love you both, don't you—"

"Great, that's great, Mom. Goodnight."

Peter hung up, head pounding.

Not surprisingly, dinner again awaited him when he got home from work the next day. But The Shape was nowhere to be seen.

Peter was feeling more than a little low. He tossed his briefcase on the sofa—the same ratty sofa he'd had back in his old apartment—and sat down to eat. Linguini today, with a nice tangy pesto sauce, fresh garlic bread and glazed carrots. Delicious. But he found himself picking at it, and pushed it away half finished. His head ached and he felt dizzy and weak.

In the living room, he noticed that the ratty sofa wasn't quite the same. Someone, The Shape no doubt, had covered it with a nice new forest green spread that actually made the whole room look a million times better. Peter didn't know where the spread had come from, but he shrugged and plopped down on it.

He grabbed the latest Entertainment Weekly off the coffee table, stretched out and started to read.

The Shape materialized near the front door and Peter barely glanced up from his magazine. He said, "Hello," and went back to the article on Lindsay Lohan's latest emotional disaster. The Shape glided toward him, grumbling low.

…Petey…

"It's Peter, remember? I'm pretty sure I mentioned that to you. I don't like being called Petey, okay?"

…Petey…

The Shape loomed over him, and, before he knew what was happening it had enveloped him in blackness and lifted him off the sofa.

"Hey!" he said, feeling himself being carried effortlessly across the living room. "Hey, what are you doing? Put me down!"

The Shape did put him down, in the cushioned armchair by the window. It set him down gently and moved away.

Peter sat in amazement for a long minute, staring as The Shape hovered in the middle of the living room. The Shape only grumbled and vibrated and Peter couldn't determine its mood.

He stood up, glaring, strolled across the living room and sat back down on the sofa where he'd been.

The Shape again swooped down on him, lifted him off the sofa and carried him back to the chair.

…Petey…, it rumbled.

Peter set his jaw angrily. He said, "This is my house, and that is my sofa. I'll sit on it if I damn well please." He stood up again and started back toward the sofa.

As he was about to sit down, The Shape lunged at him and a long black appendage shot out and batted him roughly on the side of the head.

Peter stumbled against the sofa, almost fell. The blow hadn't hurt, really, but it shocked the hell out of him and he stared in disbelief as The Shape pulsed and grumbled before him, as if daring him to try it again. The arm-like appendage was poised to slap him, maybe harder this time.

"Okay," Peter said. "Okay." He backed away until the chair was behind him, and then sat down in it very gently. "The chair it is."

The Shape, apparently gratified, glided over and petted him on the head.

"Peter," Mr. Evans said. "I'm going to get right to this, since I'm sure you wouldn't appreciate me beating around the bush."

Evans had called him in to his office only a few minutes before five o'clock and it didn't take a genius to figure out where it was going. Damn, Peter thought. I'll be damned. And today of all days, when I'm feeling like absolute crap.

"We've been doing some downsizing, as you know, and some of our more long-term positions have been outsourced to India and China. You know how that goes—"

Outsourced, Peter thought. Outsourced, just like Jenna had said. His head hurt horribly.

"It makes more economic sense for our accounting positions to go to the… well, the lowest bidder, if you will. It's work that doesn't really require good English skills, if you know what I'm saying." Evans laughed shortly before catching himself and getting back to the gravitas the situation required. "In short, Peter, I'm afraid we have to let you go."

Peter coughed and saw black spots dancing. He said, "But I'm… I've been with the company for twelve years."

Evans looked at him, as if wondering what that statement had to do with anything. He said again, "Outsourcing, you know. Effective immediately. Downturn in the economy, you understand, it's unavoidable."

Peter heard the whine in his voice when he said, "So… so the whole accounting department is being… let go?"

Evans hurrumphed uncomfortably and said, "Well, not exactly, Peter. Some of the more… industrious employees, if you will, will be staying on. Our 'forward thinkers'. Our 'take charge' types. But cuts have to happen, it's nothing personal, I'm sure you know that."

Peter said, "Who… who else is being fired?"

"Being fired, Peter, that's such a negative spin to put on it. No one's being fired. It's just downsizing, that's all."

"Okay. Who's being downsized?"

Evans looked resentful, as if Peter was ruining his entire day. Grimacing, he said, "Just you, Peter. Just you."

Peter arrived home to find that his dinner was nowhere to be seen.

The kitchen table was bare. He stared at it for a long minute, feeling his irritation rise. He threw his briefcase on the floor, tore off his tie and whipped it across the room. Typical, he thought. Typical.

He said, "Hello? Hey, where are you?"

No answer.

He stomped across the kitchen and stood in front of the refrigerator—the refrigerator he hadn't actually opened himself in several days—and said, "Hey! Where the hell are you? Where's my damn dinner, huh?"

His temples pounded so hard he felt he might vomit, and that only made him angrier. "Hey!" he screamed. "I'm calling you! Where the hell are you, and where's my goddamn dinner?"

He slammed his fists against the refrigerator, pounded his feet on the floor. "Yoo-hoo! Goddamnit, I'm home and I want my goddamn dinner now!"

Out of nowhere The Shape appeared and black anger rolled off it in waves and Peter had just enough time to think oh crap before it was on him.

It whacked him hard on the side of the head, knocking him against the refrigerator. He put up his hands to ward off the next blow, but it got him in the side, knocking out his breath, and he fell to the floor and started to scramble away. The Shape kicked at him, glancing painfully off his thigh as he scurried out of the kitchen and down the hall.

The Shape gave chase, growling and grumbling angrily. Peter half-ran, half- stumbled down the hall to the bedroom with The Shape right at his heels. It swiped at him again, stinging his buttocks, before he made it into the bedroom and dove headfirst under the bed.

The Shape lingered for a moment, its anger palpable and frightening. Peter cowered under the bed, breathing hard, so overcome with terror he could hardly think. The Shape had never shown that sort of behavior before, that sort of violent wrath.

But then again, he realized, I'd never shown that sort of behavior before.

The Shape moved away, slowly, and Peter watched it go, and his fear gave way quite suddenly to shame.

He finally got up the courage, about an hour later, to come out from under the bed. He found The Shape in the living room, near the spread-covered sofa. Meekly, Peter approached it.

The Shape's mood seemed neutral.

Peter came to it, head-down, and settled himself in at its feet. After a moment, The Shape began stroking his head, very gently, and Peter was so grateful he nearly cried.

After a few minutes, The Shape moved into the kitchen and made his dinner.

Peter spent most of his time sitting in the chair that had been designated as his, staring out the window and enjoying the warmth of the sun as it streamed through the glass. Sometimes he would get up, stretch, and wander aimlessly around the house. The Shape was often absent, but Peter didn't wonder much about where it went—as long as it returned eventually.

A few times, early on, the doorbell would ring and Peter would run away from the window and hide in the bedroom, but it didn't take long for the visitors to stop coming.

And that was good. He wasn't the most sociable of guys to begin with, and now the very thought of having to deal with other people was practically intolerable.

He took long naps and bathed often and ate the snacks The Shape left out for him and sat in the sun by the window and everything was good. At night, The Shape would come back from wherever it had been and make him a wonderful dinner and stroke his head.

Peter loved The Shape very much. The highlight of his day was invariably when The Shape returned.

But he wasn't feeling well and hadn't felt well in some time now. The headaches would come and go and sometimes they were so bad he couldn't help himself, he would vomit all over the floor. The first time The Shape had come home to this it had gone nearly insane, smacking him mercilessly and chasing him into the closet. But the second time, and the third time, The Shape's reaction changed and it seemed to be concerned. It began treating him with a bit more tenderness, altering his diet and crunching pills up into his dinner.

It didn't help. Peter was getting worse.

One afternoon, he woke up in the hallway and didn't remember how he'd gotten there. His head felt raw and he saw that he'd vomited all over himself, and the vomit was tinged red with blood.

Oh man, he thought. The Shape's gonna kill me when it sees this. But he only lay there in the hallway, too weak to move.

Sometime later The Shape arrived and Peter sensed its horror. Not anger, not in the least, but dread and worry.

Well, he thought. That's okay, I guess.

He was drifting in and out of consciousness and the world tasted like blood. He felt himself being lifted up, off the floor, saw the ceiling moving past, and pressed his head into The Shape's breast. It felt good and soft and safe.

He drifted out for a long time.

When he came to, the world was spotted with black and red and the pain in his head was unbearable. He was crying. The

Shape still held him, tenderly, and its warmth was nice but did nothing to help the horrible agony in his skull.

And then another Shape reared up in his peripheral vision, another Shape just like his Shape, another formless mass of disconnected black.

He was between the two of them, and their sadness threatened to overcome him. He felt horrible that it was he, apparently, causing this heartache, and he wanted to apologize. But he couldn't form the words.

They were speaking to each other, the weird low grumbling and vibrating sounds, and Peter found, through his pain, he could understand bits and pieces.

He heard sick, and prolonged agony.

He felt The Shape's tears, splashing against his upturned face. Don't cry, he thought. No, now, don't do that…

He heard *let him go now* and *it's time*.

He felt the needle, hot like a thin sliver of fire, slide into his neck.

His thoughts turned, very briefly, to Mom and Dad. To Jenna and Mr. Evans, brother Jeff, even Chuck and Rich, and he felt only a vague connection to them now. No, the only one who mattered was The Shape and he was sorry to leave but it was okay. He was a good boy.

Petey closed his eyes, smiling, and drifted off to that place where, in the end, all good pets go.

Made in the USA
Columbia, SC
18 February 2021